"Faria's Whisper Cove series blends compelling suspense with an engaging romance!"

~New York Times bestselling author,
Virna DePaul

Rochelle ~
Thank you for
your wonderful
friendship & sharing
your writing secrets xo
Cyndi Faria

SPIRIT AWAKENED

Whisper Cove Series, Book 1
(Prequel to Book 2, Spirit Released)

CYNDI FARIA

Even in the darkness, the light shines...

TITLES BY CYNDI FARIA

Whisper Cove Series
Spirit Awakened (Book 1)
Spirit Released (Book 2)
Spirit Embraced (Book 3)
Spirit Returned (Book 4)
Spirit Freed (Book 5)

Safe Haven Novella Series
Keep the Promise (Book 1)
Remember the Promise (Book 2)
Honor the Promise (Book 3)
Promises Collection (Books 1-3)

Visit Cyndi online at www.cyndifaria.com.

DEDICATION

To Joe, whose quest for life without boundaries inspires me.

I love you, Mom.

"What person knows a man's thoughts except
the spirit of the man which is in him?"
–Corinthians 2.11

ONE

DR. JAKE MITCHELL traversed the basement hospital maze, shaking off the chill that wormed its way down his spine. Happened every time he passed the morgue, and naturally, his pace quickened. But, as the new neurosurgeon at Full Sail Medical that rode the hilltop overlooking the rumor-haunted town of Whisper Cove, he didn't have time to address legends when he'd been hired to save lives.

Upon rounding the bend, he spotted his superior and strolled toward him. Out of respect for the chief, he had to proceed with caution because, though his hands tightened on the patient folder that held information the chief would no doubt ask for, Jake didn't believe his request would be approved.

Chief Luis Vizcaino, a stocky sixty-year-old, jabbed his index finger into his palm repeatedly while the nurse he spoke with stood with her hands on her hips and her lips pursed.

Captivated by her shimmering blonde hair and her heated blue gaze that reminded him of a pre-dawn sunrise, he shuddered with the wave of warmth blazing over him, through him. Quickly, he doused the reaction by refocusing on his case.

"Ah, Jake, just who I was looking for."

"Chief"—he nodded to the nurse but forced his gaze not to linger by pinching his eyes with his thumb and forefinger—"I'd like to talk to you about one of my patients, Tori Dawn."

With a slight hand wave, the chief gestured to the nurse. "Sure. But first, I'd like to introduce you to Nurse Cabrillo. Faith will be aiding you in future surgeries."

Accepting his offered hand, she squeezed, her petite frame the type that wouldn't crowd his space during delicate open-brain surgery. "Nice to meet you. Look forward to having your support." He faced his superior, squaring his stance and meeting those copper-tinged eyes. "Tori has come to the hospital twice in one week. She's complaining about headaches, blurred vision, and dizziness. I've already run an MRI. Extensive blood work. Everything came back normal, so I sent her home. I'd like to get your approval to perform exploratory surgery."

Adjusting his lab coat, the chief blew out a breath. "We don't perform exploratory surgery at Full Sail Medical on a hunch, Dr. Mitchell."

With a narrowed gaze, Jake pulled back. He didn't trust his instincts. Not any longer... "This isn't a hunch." He handed the folder to the chief. "Proving or disproving what the MRI doesn't show can only be accomplished through surgery."

As if the chief had heard such requests previously, he ran a slow hand over his face. Then he flipped through several pages, pausing to examine the MRI results. "At this time, you've shown no evidence surgery is warranted. Run more tests. Maybe send her to an ENT."

"An ear, nose, and throat specialist sent her to *me*." Jake jutted his chin and his brows lowered. "But there's more." He leaned in, his shoulders bridging the gap between the chief and Faith. Her floral scent filled his lungs and caused him to peer at her for an instant. "For the past week, five other patients have complained of similar symptoms—some are reporting they are hearing voices—with inconclusive test results, and this could indicate a potential health crisis."

Shuffling his weight from one foot to another, the chief stepped back and held Jake's gaze. "As far as we know, these other patients are doing fine. They haven't returned, correct?"

"They're not doing fine. They're hearing voices." As soon as he repeated the words, an eerie feeling buzzed through him. He fought to silence his jittery nerves. Intuition had no place in his world when patients depended on his science. Still, something wasn't right here. He squirmed in his scrubs and yanked the collar forward. "It's true no patients have returned, but—"

"Tori is the mayor's daughter," Faith interjected, her hand coming to rest on Jake's upper arm before swiftly retracting. "She's more outspoken. Persistent."

Glancing at where Faith had touched his arm, Jake then met her consuming gaze. Those keen blue eyes reminded him of his aunt, who'd raised him…the dear aunt he'd watched die on the operating table. He shivered. The loss still shook him to the core. Losing a patient always hurt, but the loss of his beloved family member tore him apart. He swallowed hard. "Regardless of Tori's title, I'm obligated to keep searching for answers. This hospital is obligated."

Chief scoffed, shook his head, and then glared. "Jake, you're a man of facts. So am I. Until you have evidence of a problem, let this go."

For a moment, he was tempted to listen to his superior, but then the hairs at the back of his neck rose—as if he were walking through the dark forest on a moonless night…the same creepiness he felt when passing the basement morgue. "I need your approval. My findings could potentially guide me to discover what's happening in this town…."

The chief held up a finger. "Don't be an alarmist, Dr. Mitchell. Tori hasn't returned. Until she seeks medical help, let's hope her vague symptoms dissipate organically."

He shoved both hands in his pockets. His first month at the hospital and, more than anything, he wanted to earn his superior's approval and pass probation in order to make Whisper Cove his home. How else would he someday transition from the demands of a surgeon to offering his skills inside a community clinic, like the one he'd been treated at as a kid?

"You hired me for my expertise, not intuition. If she returns, I'll run more tests."

"Good." The chief gave a firm nod.

"Everyone has to rely on his own intuition at sometime in his or her life," Faith argued. "Could be your time now, couldn't it?"

His head whipped toward Faith, who'd been silent so long he'd almost forgotten she was there. Almost. Then he pinned his stare on his superior, who turned to look at Faith with a glare that caused her to glance at her feet. "We can't avoid the obvious." He tapped his chin. "Faith's right. Something is going on with Tori I need to lock down."

"Right or not." Chief cleared his throat and folded his arms. "With malpractice on the rise, we want to make sure every diagnosis and test result is documented before we go running blind into surgery. Or we'll all be searching for new careers."

At his superior's threatening tone, Jake huffed. He needed to proceed with caution. One wrong decision could cost him his career in lawsuits and legal fees.

Chief thrust the folder at Jake, who reluctantly accepted. "I can't authorize open-brain surgery until Tori's condition warrants specific treatment. End of discussion." He nodded at Faith and then sauntered away.

Jake gazed at Faith, not because he was looking for input, but because the conversation couldn't have been comfortable. "I'm sorry you had to hear that."

She shrugged and turned her head to the side. "It's a sticky situation. You want to save lives, and that's my goal, too. But, I think you're right…now and again we have to look past what can be seen and listen to that little voice. As a man of science, I can't imagine that would be easy for you."

The corner of his mouth tipped upward, and he strolled toward the cafeteria.

Faith followed.

Maybe he'd grab a Vitamin Water or a coffee, something that might stimulate his mind and provide the answers he needed. "No, listening to my intuition is not easy. But, I'm right on Tori's account. Something doesn't add up."

"Have you ever felt like you've needed to do exploratory surgery before?"

Faith's upturned face, her sky-blue irises

ringed by a dark circle, matched the way he felt inside—hopeful, but trapped by policy and insurance stipulations. Now, his superior wanted him to shelf his "feelings".

Facts had never let him down, though. However, in regard to Faith's question, he didn't want to burden her with the details of his past. "Not like this."

"Okay." She popped her shoulder. "What's different this time?"

He paused, coming to a stop in the center of the hallway. He glanced down at Faith. The woman was unbelievably attractive in that California blonde-haired, blue-eyed way, although her skin lacked the sun-kissed tan from living in a coastal town that seemed to have more foggy days than sunny ones. "Here's the thing, Faith. Tori is not the only patient complaining of neck pain, nausea, and light sensitivity. How can five patients with the exact same symptoms be a coincidence?"

She tapped her chest. "You're the specialist, and I think you should trust yourself."

"We rely on test results, but at some point, the patient is the one who knows his or her own body best. We have to listen to that." He sank his hand in his pocket, palmed his aunt's ring—his version of a worry stone—and ran his thumb over the smooth surface. The ring was the only remnant he had left of the woman who'd raised him, of his family. He glanced in the direction the chief had gone. "It's an uneasy balance, taking that into account."

Again, she reached out and touched his arm. "Don't give up. You should talk to the chief again."

Tingling from her gentle touch, he tapped his foot, the sole making a *rap-rap-rap* sound on the tiled floor. Could he connect both facts and intuition, learn to trust his gut feeling again, and possibly allow that sensation to lead him to healing his patient? With this being Jake's first month at Full Sail, a disastrous mistake could cost someone their life—not something Jake ever took lightly. But, he wanted to cure his patients, all of them, and continue to heal the residents of Whisper Cove. He loved this quaint coastal town he wanted to call home, and he wouldn't give up his oath to help those in need. But, other than his patients' claims, he didn't have any evidence, so maybe the chief was right. The well-respected elder owned the hospital and was a legend among neurosurgeons. *No.* For the time being, he thought so highly of Chief Vizcaino, he needed to respect the man. "Chief has more experience than me. What he recommends, I have to follow—"

Tori appeared in the hallway, her palm flat against the corridor wall as she held herself upright. She inched her hand along the painted block wall to keep her balance, but stumbled. When she spotted Jake, her brown eyes suddenly widened, her face turned ashen, and she slid to the floor.

Adrenaline surged through his muscles, and he rushed toward her. Before she hit her head against the floor, he caught her in his arms. In the background, he could hear Faith call for assistance.

Those precious minutes after Tori had collapsed turned to hours. Now, based on the results of the new MRI, Jake ordered her into surgery. While he scrubbed in, he addressed his senior. "Exploratory surgery would have caught the aneurysm before it burst. I think we need to discuss a policy change."

"There was no way to foresee this." The chief leaned against the counter, his gaze meeting Jake's. "Her MRI came back clean. Blood work was normal. That's hospital practice, and some incidents are out of our control. When this is over, we need to talk." He headed into the observation room.

Jake swallowed his irritation and willed his mind and body to calm before he headed into surgery. Once inside, he glanced to the team, their hospital blues the only hint of color inside the white, sterile room. The anesthesiologist stood just to his left, Faith across from him, and another nurse prepared his supplies. He adjusted his facemask, palmed the scalpel, and allowed his exhalation to flow out steadily as he set to save Tori's life, a wife and mother of young son.

An hour into the surgery, Faith lifted a damp cloth and, in gentle strokes, blotted Jake's tacky forehead.

Her touch bathed his body in gooseflesh he couldn't ignore, but shook off. For Tori, he had to be focused. Absolutely focused in order to return her to her loved ones. To her son.

Keeping up with the procedure, Faith exchanged one instrument for another, her experience in the operating room apparent.

However, the cloth mask Jake wore covered

his flattened lips, as the gown did the ache in his chest. Because he knew firsthand the ramifications of losing a mother…

But, even as Jake began to seal the vein, inside his gut, his mind, something still felt wrong—

"Close her up, Dr. Mitchell." The chief's voice echoed through the ceiling speakers.

Jake flicked his gaze to the glass in the background where his superior stood then looked down at the surgery site, his hand suspended above the clip he'd placed at the base of the aneurysm. He let out a breath. *Chief is right. Your work is complete*—

An alarm sounded, the shrill noise jacking Jake's heart-rate into his throat. He jerked his glare to the anesthesiologist then lowered it to where his hand hovered.

Blood pooled.

A second hemorrhage that had been previously hidden.

"Pressure is dropping. Heart rate is erratic." The anesthesiologist called out the stats.

"What's happening?" Chief's request for information matched Jake's hunt for answers.

Since the MRI hadn't shown either

aneurysm, Jake manually spread the brain tissue in search of a second bleed. Only the bulbous leaking vein wasn't there, or it was too small to make out, too deep. "Dr. Vizcaino, I need your assistance."

When the chief didn't answer, Jake curled over Tori, adjusted his headgear, and mumbled to himself, "I can't find the bleed…"

"You've got this, Dr. Mitchell." Faith's voice was calm and should've been soothing. "Keep looking."

His thundering pulse raged in his ears.

More of that tender blotting happened along his forehead.

"Three minutes. I can't regulate her blood pressure. We're going to lose her if you don't make this quick." The anesthesiologist's voice trembled.

Fingers spreading the delicate tissue, Jake narrowed his glare. Heart pounding, heat boring down his spine, he probed. Faith's words repeated inside his mind like his aunt's gentle encouragements that were always in the background and kept him focused on the path ahead. Of successful surgeries and saving lives. "I'm not telling her husband he's raising his son alone."

"Four minutes…"

The time for irreversible brain damage from lack of oxygen encroaching, he cursed.

Why in the hell was the chief taking so long to scrub in?

Prickly heat darted across Jake's skin, and hints of doubt began to creep in. But he wouldn't give up. Couldn't.

The door flew wide and the chief entered, but didn't call out instructions like Jake expected. Maybe it was time to move aside and have someone step in. "Chief?"

At the chief's silence, Jake jerked up his head and witnessed his superior and Faith sharing another look with some meaning that escaped him.

"You can do this, Dr. Mitchell." Faith applied suction then handed him another instrument. "Trust yourself. That's it…"

Those encouraging words circled around him, inside his mind, though they seemed to echo within the room. His aunt had absolutely believed in his abilities to become a neurosurgeon. He needed to trust in those abilities now.

Jake remained a solid force over Tori and mashed his lips tight to keep his frustration corralled. The bleed was there, but how did his instincts penetrate what he couldn't physically locate?

"Time's running out…" the anesthesiologist urged.

"Keep searching. Don't give up. You're here for a reason." Faith adjusted the overhead light, her cap brushing his from across the table. "To the left, below the vein stem…."

Static razored across his forearms, as if an ethereal force commanded his fingers to locate the second, grain-sized bulge in the vein just where Faith had suggested. But, the hemorrhage was tiny enough that only through exploratory surgery would he have found the location. Trusting Faith's instincts, he worked to return mother to son.

"Got it." From beside him, the elder's voice resonated in approval.

A cold chill darted through him. If he didn't learn to stand up for his intuition and trust his own instincts, he'd never become the doctor patients trusted and depended on, befriended and remembered, flooded his future clinic for his support.

With nimble hands, Faith used the aspirator to clean the tissue then offered him the needed instrument to help seal the bleed.

All the tools presented were essential to save Tori's life. With Faith working beside him like an extension of himself, he stopped the hemorrhage and completed the surgery. A half-hour later, he watched as Tori headed to recovery, his body humming with awareness he both wanted to keep in remission, yet fully explore.

By trusting Faith, Jake *had* saved Tori's life.

Yet, who was Faith Cabrillo? How had she known where the aneurysm resided when he, as a neurosurgeon, had not? Unless the chief didn't believe Tori could be saved, why else had he held back assistance during the touch-and-go surgery? As if they both possessed a sixth sense, what was the meaning of the look that passed between the chief and Faith before she informed Jake the exact location of the hemorrhage?

His very soul resisted accepting the impossible.

Standing in the hallway, staff members coursing around him like water around a boulder that split a river, his conflict over whether to leave facts behind and travel to the shore of intuition narrowed. What he'd been searching for caused his feet to pivot toward the center of the surgery unit, where Faith sat at the nurses' hub. He met her gaze briefly before she looked away. Her kindness and belief in him unlocked a well of memories, of warmth and tenderness, and an image of what home looked like…something he so desperately wanted again, along with a partner he could share his future vision with.

Suddenly, Jake had one thought: Whether Faith knew it or not, she'd saved a life today. How strange how that life felt like his own.

"Jake's looking at you. What are you going to do?"

Faith shook her head just as Patti Woodward, the second assisting surgery nurse and Faith's good friend, leaned against the station counter with her eyebrows peaked over sandy-brown eyes. After a painful breakup, no matter how handsome the dark-haired, hazel-eyed doctor was, no matter how her tummy fluttered when he stared in her direction, the last thing she wanted was to draw the attention of a man when she had finally reclaimed her stability. "I'm not *doing* anything. Dr. Mitchell saved a life. That's his job. I assisted. I'm finalizing my paperwork and heading home to enjoy the weekend—replanting my window boxes."

Low brows shadowed Patti's eyes. "You don't have window boxes."

Faith sighed. "I can't fool you."

The counter jiggled and Patti bent down. "Nope. But, I wasn't the only one who saw the look between you and Chief Vizcaino. What was that all about?"

Stiffening her spine, she had hoped no one other than the chief noticed her alarm. One second, Jake was requesting help, and the next, a womanly silhouette, her translucent form—a true Fog Spirit—appeared. Both Faith and Chief Vizcaino were from Founding Families and bound by the Whisper Cove curse. All Founding Family members could both see and hear spirits, and she'd learned from childhood to keep her ability to see the dead hidden. "Nothing."

"That's your answer?" Patti palmed the

counter.

At Patti's incredulous look, Faith rolled a shoulder. "It was a look. A plea. I was concerned about Tori, and from my angle, I could see what Jake could not. Plain and simple."

"I think there's more to what you're telling me. By the way Jake is still standing in the hallway staring, he does, too. And, I saw how determined he was to save Tori…he won't easily dismiss whatever was going on between you and the chief. Or the fact that you aided him in surgery." Patti reached out and took Faith's hand. "There was a Fog Spirit in the room, wasn't there?"

Faith eased her hand from Patti's and stared at her empty ring finger. A curse was hurled upon couples—a Lover's Curse. She'd witnessed firsthand the damage that loving her caused. Her ex-fiancé was now blind, and his dream of composing music ruined. She couldn't allow anyone to be interested in her again. Though Patti knew about The Curse, even with her bestie, Faith was forbidden by the Founding Counsel to confirm the existence of spirits. She forced a smile that didn't pinch her eyes. "Don't be silly. There's no such thing as Fog Spirits.

That's only what parents tell their children to keep them in line."

Patti exhaled slowly, pulled out a chair, and plopped down. "Whatever." She flipped her hand. "You can't lie to me, Faith. But, you need to think of a better response quickly, because Jake is headed this way. Something tells me he's not going to accept 'nothing' for an answer."

Those flutters in Faith's tummy punched at her insides. Out of the corner of her eye, she glanced to see Jake striding her way. Even in scrubs, Jake's fitness was undeniable. The powder-blue cotton pulled tight across his shoulders and the half-sleeves strained to conceal his upper arms—a sight that sent a heat-filled ripple straight through her belly.

Patti sighed. "I'd tell him anything. He's gorgeous."

Ducking below the counter, Faith gaped at her friend. "Patti, you're in a serious relationship," she scolded.

"And very happy. That's what I want for you." She tossed her head in Jake's direction. "You should talk to him."

Daring a second look, Faith rose to see the sexy doctor had been stopped by the anesthesiologist. "He's busy."

"Don't you read the schedule?" Patti rolled her eyes. "He has his first weekend off in a month. After *that* surgery, he probably needs to unload before he can enjoy the next two days. The least you can do is make him feel comfortable while he's here. You do have to work with him."

Barely raising her head, Faith spied over the counter to see him stalk toward her, only to be stopped again by an orderly pushing a wheelchair, so the seated Ms. Wilson could talk to Jake.

Patti bumped Faith's shoulder. "Ms. Wilson's only visitor is the pastor on Sunday afternoons."

Faith scrunched her brows. She peeled off her surgical cap and tossed it into the laundry waste bin just as a pang of sadness rippled through her. She didn't want to age alone, though she wasn't about to admit that to Patti. How amazing would it be to grow old with someone as passionate and compassionate as Jake? "And Ms. Wilson is smiling…"

"Could be gas…" Patti slid into her chair. "Maybe ask him to coffee."

Scowling, even though Patti was right, she rebutted, "I don't drink coffee. You know that."

"Okay. Tea, whatever…" Patti flashed both palms then spun to face the counter. Her fingers settled on her keyboard. "You're worth loving, that's all I'm saying."

Faith's last romance had begun with Arabica roast, two sugars, and cream. She didn't plan on sharing that type of romantic intimacy with another man. With the back of her hand, she wiped her mouth. She hadn't touched the stuff in nearly two years since her wedding day fiasco. She sighed.

Patti paused from typing. "You'll never break The Curse if you don't take a chance on love."

Shuddering, Faith recalled her wedding day disaster. Townspeople claimed she was left at the altar, but brides don't get abandoned at the pulpit. *Uh uh.* That awful event became clear as a spring day. Through the mission church's double doors she had entered the sanctuary, beheld the illumination of 200 piercing stares, and pieced together the murmurs Steven Silva had changed his mind.

Moments later, Faith's wedding day glow

turned an ashen grey. At least, she assumed the blood drained from her face before she fainted. She woke on the aisle floor, dress bunched around her knees. Her mother crouched beside her, rosy cheeks smeared with mascara, and fanned Faith with a leather-bound bible. She learned later on that very day Steven had mysteriously lost his eyesight. Her love, The Curse, and his betrayal had swiftly struck him down.

That was the day she'd sworn off coffee because she'd begun her relationship by sharing a steaming cup of brew with Steven. The night before her wedding, during the rehearsal, she'd actually raised her coffee cup and *clinked* the porcelain mug with Steven's to celebrate the future. "I'm going home." She gathered her soft lunch cooler bag and slipped her cell phone inside the side pocket along with her car keys.

"Faith." Jake stood at the counter, his hazel eyes—deep, mysterious pools—connecting with her gaze. "I need to talk to you."

Tremors rippled through her. Glancing to the side, Faith saw Patti shuffling paperwork. She inhaled an unsteady breath, her eyelids blinking too fast. "What do you need, Doctor?"

"I think you know." He pushed his forearms across the narrow counter. "Can we go somewhere private?"

"I'm about to leave." She frowned apologetically. "We can talk on Monday, if that's okay."

He slid his arms off the counter and massaged the back of his neck. "This is business, and I'm afraid it can't wait. But if you're about to leave, let's get a cup of coffee."

Patti cleared her throat and mumbled, "Told you…"

Faith glared at Patti then turned back around. "Coffee's not business."

"It is if we have it in the break-room." The scent of his spiced cologne wafted around the nurses' hub.

Faith held her breath. She didn't want to spend time alone with him unless she had to, not with his intoxicating scent and deep voice that vibrated places… She stood and the chair rolled back until it collided with the adjoining station. "Sorry, but the break-room is for off-work time."

"You're trying to avoid me." His gaze narrowed and he tapped the counter with an index finger. "But it won't work."

"No, no, I'm not avoiding you." Suddenly feeling the burn of his gaze hot on her cheeks, she unbuttoned her smock a half-inch. "Really."

Elbows on the counter, he slid toward her. "Then let's talk. Now."

$\mathcal{T}$WO

INSIDE THE SMALL break room, the snack station was sandwiched between a counter, sink, coffee area, and a personnel refrigerator. Two nurses were chatting at the center table, so Jake motioned for Faith to sit at the corner table away from them. "How do you take your coffee?"

She folded her hands in her lap and subtly shook her head. "I don't drink the stuff. At least, not any longer."

He furrowed his brows. "Water, then?"

"If this is a business meeting, can we proceed, Dr. Mitchell? I'm off in ten minutes."

Anxious to talk, he dismissed the coffee. Pulling out the plastic chair, he glanced around the room. He sat so he could stare into her wide, impatient eyes.

Those fingers of hers laced together and she

vibrated one leg, like she was nervous.

He set his hands on the table and tee-peed his index fingers. "How did you know where the aneurysm was located?" She paused to seeming gather her words.

"You'd have found the problem more quickly if your search for facts hadn't distracted your intuition."

Startled by her declaration of the truth, Jake darted his gaze to the door. "You didn't answer my question."

She shoved back her chair, ready to stand. "From where I was on the opposite side of the table, I-I could see blood pumping."

Stomach clenching, Jake rolled shoulders that tensed with a blanket of unease, because he knew Faith was lying. "I think there's more than that. You exchanged a look with the chief. Why?"

She shrugged a shoulder. "This is ridiculous. You're the expert, and I was simply assisting. I don't appreciate the interrogation."

"Then answer my question, and we'll be done."

Another employee entered the room and put change into the snack machine that responded with a *clank*.

When the employee left, Jake continued talking in a low voice. He held her gaze and watched for her pupils to dilate or constrict, or for her to simply turn away. "How did you know where the bleed was located?"

Faith pushed to her feet.

No, she can't leave yet. He grabbed her hand to keep her from leaving. But, seeing her glare at his grasp, he released her.

She stared down at him. "We worked together. Saved Tori. That's all that should matter in this case." She palmed her heart, letting her fingers tap over the button-down V in her collar. "Saving people is what matters to me, and that's what should matter to you, as well. How about you just thank me for my help and we move on?"

The passion in her eyes, her curvy body suddenly stiffening with conviction, her vigor, caused him to quiver. He didn't want to get involved with someone he couldn't trust, no matter how damn attractive Faith's determination to keep information from him was. During his internship, he'd given his heart to Lexi, only to return to an empty apartment and a note telling him she reunited with her ex. Blindsided, he had found comfort in his work, healing others in lieu of wallowing in her betrayal. That's why he needed to focus on the facts now and keep his attraction hidden. "I agree, saving people is top priority. However, I'm trying to figure out how to repeat that miracle you performed in surgery today." He leaned forward. "So, you must tell me."

She tipped her head and briefly closed her eyes. "Fate stood with us and guided us both. Nothing more…" She glanced toward the empty corner booth and her eyes flashed wide before meeting his gaze.

In regards to his discussion with her, as fierce as his will to hunt for the answer became, he determined she fought as hard to keep something secret.

A stalemate that he needed to stay clear of. If only the way she nibbled on her lip, and her blue stare, didn't have him reaching forward to where her hand touched the table to be near her, so he could feel the heat roll off her skin. "I can get fixated on making connections…"

"I've answered your question. Looks like you're stuck working with me, regardless of whether you accept the answer was Fate." She glanced toward the other nurses, who were still chatting. "As tenacious as Chief Vizcaino is with us working as a team, I'm going to challenge that until I'm placed back in pediatrics."

"Pediatrics." He leaned back in the chair. "Tell me more. What other departments have you worked in? Your reason for working here?"

She glanced to the waiting chair and sat, adding a sigh. In that pent-up-energy way a leg moves when a person wants to be anywhere but where they are forced to stay, her leg began to jiggle. "I'm really not that interesting." She pulled the stainless steel napkin holder toward her. "I've lived here all of my life and worked at this hospital for the past six years." She spun the napkin container. "For a time in the lab, I studied rhizomes and their healing powers."

"Really?" He smiled. They had a common interest. "I wrote my thesis on neurotoxins found in the iris bulb." He rubbed his chin and leaned inward, her floral scent once again causing him to breathe deeply. "Greek mythology says the goddess Iris is the mother of love."

"Is that right…?" In her grasp, the napkin

holder stilled. "We have a saying in the lab, well, actually it's Chief's declaration. He says, 'The bloom lies in the hands of the propagator'." She wobbled her shoulder and her brows tipped down. "I think it means each of us has the power to change the outcome. Believing in ourselves, that's where Fate comes in."

At the way she mimicked the chief, Jake grinned, his cheeks bunching until his chest swelled. But fate, if he believed, could it bring two people together for a common goal? He recalled when he'd seen the two talking. "If you're interested in pediatrics then you're upset about the move into surgery?"

Her leg quieted and she raised a brow. "Your intuition is spot on."

At her sarcasm and his sad number of wins in the 'intuition' department, he felt like he'd been punched in the belly. Or was his gut reaction from her displeasure at working with him? Rejection when he wanted to get to know her further, what she kept hidden from him, and why. He scooted his chair forward. "Tell me more about yourself. Your family."

She smiled, her lips curling and her eyes sparkling.

That beautiful smile touched someplace deep inside, awakening a feeling—curiosity, perhaps, or compassion for another and wanting to heal what had been broken. Because though she smiled, in her eyes lay an awareness of something dark. Something he couldn't define. Yes, he definitely needed to keep away from Faith, before she sucked him into her world so deeply he'd never escape. She'd be the distraction he couldn't afford, and he needed his wits to figure out what was happening to his patients.

"I have supportive parents. The rest, I'm afraid, would only bore you." She jostled the napkin holder then pressed her finger against a place where the white paper ruffled. "What about your folks?"

"My mom died. Dad couldn't deal. My aunt raised me." He huffed at the ease which telling her his past flowed and lowered his head.

"I'm sorry."

"Don't be. You make me want to tell you everything."

She scooted closer. "Then do. What made you want to become a neurosurgeon?"

An image of his aunt floated to the surface

of his mind. She'd had that peaceful, tender way that made others gravitate toward her, similar to Faith. "Like I said, my aunt raised me. But when I was twelve, she had a stroke. Her recovery was difficult. I knew then I wanted to save others, and she supported me in that direction."

"She must be very proud of you."

Heart squeezing, he lowered his head and dropped one hand to finger the ring he kept inside his pocket. His aunt's band represented the only family he'd had, but also reminded him of the day her treating surgeon had reacted to his gut feeling and failed to save her. That's why Jake found comfort in facts. Facts had never let him down.

Until now.

Faith's hand landed on his extended arm, and she squeezed. "I apologize. I shouldn't ask such personal questions, but you started it."

He raised his head and, through a watery blur, glanced at her delicate fingers draped over his forearm. That simple gesture made him want to cover her hand with his, to fully feel the comfort a woman like Faith could give. But, at the same time, he couldn't risk being distracted by feelings he found hard to understand. Harder to recover from when those secrets she held seemed buried. He pulled his arm away. "No reason to be sorry or apologize." He exhaled and pushed to stand. "I'll talk to Chief. See if I can't get you transferred back to pediatrics."

At that moment, the chief entered the room. "Nonsense."

His boisterous voice caught the attention of the other occupants, who picked up their trays and hurried out of the room.

"Communication. Teambuilding is top priority. Part of Full Sail Medical's Value Statement. And you're my Dream Team." He dug in his coat pocket, pulled out two tickets, and handed each of them one. "You need to work as a cohesive unit, permanently."

"Permanently?" With wide eyes, Jake stared down at his ticket then his head sprang up, his eyes widening even more. "A Zip Line Couples Encounter is your answer to testing if I'm a team player?"

Faith's mouth hung open, and she jolted to her feet. "*Dream Team…Couples Encounter…*Now, Chief, you're going too far."

The chief pinned Faith with a hard stare that she met.

At the awkward stare-down, Jake cleared his throat. "What's going on between you?"

Chief ignored Jake, just like before in the OR, and spoke directly to her. "Faith, Jake's livelihood, involving teamwork for the good of the hospital, depends on *you*."

Again, she retreated. "Dr. Mitchell's livelihood doesn't depend on anyone but *him*."

A flash of discomfort made him jolt. "Hey, I'm standing right here." He palmed his hips and rocked his jaw. "Faith assisted me and did a fine job. That's exactly the kind of teammate I'm looking for. Someone I can trust. But, I can't risk relying on her if she's not committed 100%. Her desire is to return to pediatrics."

"Pediatrics has plenty of other staff. She belongs here, with you. You can't deny you trusted her just fine. Saved Tori's life. In the future, you'll save more lives."

Cheeks flushing, Faith massaged her face. "Well, there's no reason for a two-day 'Encounter'"—she waved her ticket—"when we can appease your requirements by aiding patients here."

"Trust me. I've sent other teams before. Couple's Encounter's method is proven."

Chief's gaze met his. "A few hours per week in surgery together isn't enough to fuse what could be the Dream Team I've been hoping to again offer patients. It's an exercise to develop trust."

"Chief, I don't—"

"Dr. Mitchell, hear me out." The chief raised his hand. "Faith has a connection with you I'd like to…kindle."

"Kindle?" Her voice rose until it squeaked.

Jake shuddered at her discomfort.

"Professionally, of course. For the good of the hospital." The chief's glare met hers. "Faith, there is no denying what we both witnessed. Your partnership has the possibility to become binding in a way dreams are made of."

Her hands balled at her sides, and she glanced to the empty corner booth then to the open door. "All of this talk of dreams…Be careful what you wish for…"

Brows rolling forward with concern, Jake split his gaze between the two. Surgeons were required to pass a one-year probationary period. As far as he'd seen, the chief tested boundaries not because he was as harsh as he appeared, but because he prided himself on the hospital working as a solid unit built on trust. Family.

Initially, that was the sole lure to Full Sail Medical. But, there were limits he didn't want to cross, and that included forcing someone on a team they had no intention of committing to. "Chief, she doesn't want this. Therefore, neither do I." He held out his ticket. "Thank you for the thought, but we can't accept this—"

"Wait." She exhaled, gave that corner a long stare down, and then grabbed the ticket from Jake's hand. "We'll do it. One weekend. To better serve the community, I think we can work through two days."

With her face lifted, she met his stare, those softening blue eyes locked on his in a way he could not glance away from. Again, she'd saved him. Maybe he'd get the chance to save her…her position, anyway.

Chief poked his finger at the tickets. "Well, it's settled. I suggest you both head home. Get a good night's sleep. Encounter registration begins at nine am sharp."

THREE

EIGHT HOURS LATER, Faith still battled the chief's words that ricocheted against the walls of her mind.

Jake's livelihood depends on you… Don't deny your connection…

Along with his words, she, too, wondered if her heart, if her very soul, was strong enough to risk chancing love for the second time. In the comfort of her bed, even with the sound of the sea in the distance floating in through the open window, she tossed at the memory of seeing the forlorn womanly apparition sitting in the corner booth of the break-room. Faith would never break The Curse and find eternal love, if she didn't risk opening her heart again. However, the rumbling sea was unable to override her fear of putting another man at risk of The Curse's hard ruling. Sure, she wanted to do what was good for the hospital, but she could fall for Jake—er, Dr. Mitchell—way too easily. Sigh.

In the chief's quest for his Dream Team, something told her he had found another couple to focus his matchmaking efforts on. Even more, spirits had the ability to make a fluke diagnosis or surgery seem like a miracle. In the chief's eyes, a win-win.

Or not.

The Lover's Curse had surrounded the town ever since an Ohlone shaman named Rosa had been rejected by the mission soldier she came to love. Seeking retribution, she cursed the Founding Fathers and their families to a loveless life thereafter. Some said Rosa still haunted the town in search of a way to be released.

Face down, Faith screamed her frustration into her downy pillow and prayed Rosa would find freedom soon. Faith didn't need anyone playing matchmaker with her pathetic dating life. She could not ever date Jake, so she needed to convince him she was a mess. He was intelligent, his career on the fast track, and he didn't need a woman like her who would only destroy his dreams. Shouldn't be too hard to keep a distance between them. He wasn't interested in her on a personal level. Not that she could tell.

Swinging her bare feet to the floor, she took a tired breath. She trudged to the kitchen, ruffled through a few random teabags, passing on the breakfast blend, the orange pekoe, and finally settled on chamomile while praying for peace.

Whisper Cove, however, was not a place of calm. She'd lost once and didn't want to lose again. However, as a nurse, saving lives had always been top priority and that precedent hadn't changed.

The mug with the hummingbird decal popped out at her, but as she reached upward, she noticed the dusty coffee pot. Her heart thrummed with nostalgia, not only of missing the dark roast, but of a curse-free future.

She balled the kitchen towel and tossed it at the coffee machine. The day Steven abandoned her, she should have returned the fancy engagement gift or thrown away the ugly reminder of a failed relationship.

Her lip quivered, but she bit down hard. She was done with the past. Patti was right, Faith needed to enter her future with the goal of breaking The Curse.

With an *oomph*, she hoisted the appliance into

her arms, the cord whipping along the floor, her bathrobe curled up her thighs to expose a cotton tee underneath, and headed toward the door with purpose-filled steps. She flung the front door wide and stopped cold, her eyes popping open along with her mouth.

Jake stood on the top step, the single porch light capturing the green in his hazel eyes two shades darker than his polo shirt. He held two paper cups emblazoned with the Suede's Diner insignia, similar to the one on her mug.

She kicked at the cord that twisted around her ankles, her breath rushing in and out. "How did you get my address?"

"The hospital. Actually, when I checked in on Tori, I asked Patti."

Curling her toes until her feet cramped seemed like a better way of venting than screaming. She and Patti needed to have a serious talk. "Why are you here? I mean, Dr. Mitchell—"

"Jake."

"Jake, if there is an emergency, you could have called."

With downturned eyes, he glanced behind him then nudged her welcome mat with the toe of his shoe. "I did call. The phone went to voice mail."

She glanced toward her lunch bag. Flustered as she'd been when she'd gotten home last night, she'd forgotten to remove her phone to charge it. "That still doesn't explain why you're here. It's six in the morning. We have three hours before the retreat begins."

Again, he tapped the door mat. "At the risk of sounding childish, I had a nightmare, and thought I'd heed your advice to listen to my intuition. First, I headed to the hospital to check on Tori, but she's doing well. When I saw Patti, I told her I forgot to get your address so I could pick you up for the team-building retreat. That wasn't exactly a lie."

Letting her feet relax, Faith lifted the corner of her mouth into a half-smile. Where, a moment ago, she viewed him as overstepping his position, now she considered him inspiring. She couldn't have imagined him listening to his feelings was easy. He was putting himself out there. Could she do the same? "Well, unless your dream included me fighting with an appliance, I'm fine."

With a grin threatening on his lips, he

lowered his gaze to the pot she continued to wrestle with. "In my defense, it appears the appliance is winning. That cord does look menacing, all coiled up around your feet. You could trip. Tumble head over heels."

She glared, blinking while his intoxicating cologne teased her to inhale. At that instant, with him standing there, sleeves pulled tight so the muscles were defined…*good heavens, how I could fall*. She both shivered with need and hated him. But, with bedhead attacking her hair, Faith couldn't believe he was still standing on her porch. "I don't fall easily." She pulled up the cord. "I've got this tackled. And I think it best we drive separate cars."

He wiggled the cups and tilted his head, adorably. "Fog is thickening. Invite me in, so I can try to change your mind without watching you shiver."

Change her mind about cars or chancing partnering with him? Already rising from the mist, Fog Spirits were crowding her courtyard. However, specks of maroon shimmered in Jake's eyes, like beach glass, and she inched forward, holding his tentative gaze. What were the spirits seeing in this man that she resisted?

"Go ahead, the choice is all yours."

She stared at the cups with steam rising from the holes pierced in the lids. One showed whipped cream bubbling through the top and a splash of chocolate that reminded her of simpler times when the pain of heartbreak hadn't yet burned. The other caramel-colored coffee, rich with sweet cream, caused her to practically salivate. She inhaled and released a slow breath. Could she let him inside her home, her heart? "I don't just let anyone inside. And I-I already have tea brewing."

"Let me guess…chamomile." He chuckled.

She frowned. Was she that predictable? Boring? "You got lucky." She shifted the pot's weight to rest in the crook of her arm.

His gaze painted its way down her body, pausing at the satin tie that loosely held the robe from spilling open, and his grin broadened. "I agree," he crooned and leaned against the doorjamb. "I am lucky. You're even more beautiful out of your scrubs." Suddenly, his gaze dropped. "I'm sorry. That just slipped out…"

Her heart sped and a shiver tingled across her skin. She attempted to cover her thighs and pursed her lips at the change in him. "What's going on? Seriously, a few hours ago, you were offering to move me out of your section, now you're…flirting?"

He held out the drinks. "If I told you the truth, you wouldn't believe me. But that dream didn't begin as a nightmare."

They never do. The Curse. From experience, most likely spirits were making their presence known to the newest member of Whisper Cove. However, Jake's calm eyes reminded her of tide pools where, if one looked closer, there was life, so much life inside that encouraged her to take a chance at building a relationship instead of pushing him away. "Well, the dream has faded, right?"

He met her stare and shook his head. "Quite the opposite. I am becoming more and more clear." He glanced at the machine in her arms. "You said you don't drink coffee. The hot chocolate *is* perfect temperature, 140 degrees. Might as well take it before it gets cold."

Insides twisting from coffee memories, she swallowed at the remembrance of the rich aroma, the way the cream softened the bitter jolt, the way the addition of sugar caused her eyes to close like experiencing a first kiss…sharing her morning with a man she loved. She lifted her gaze to see Jake lick his lips and his hazel stare settle on hers. Quickly juggling the pot, she looked at the coffee long and hard. *Take it, drink it down, let it fill you once again…*

"Go ahead." He pushed the coffee her way. "It's yours."

Oh, who was she kidding? Jake had an A+ in the looks and brains department. He was the first man to show interest in building something with her other than a business relationship. She swallowed, imagining the taste of so much more than a cup of joe.

"Be honest with yourself, Faith. If it's coffee you'd rather have, don't deny yourself what you really want."

Before she crossed the boundaries she'd erected to keep her heart protected, she snatched the hot chocolate and sipped. "I am honest."

His chuckle flowed across her skin, like a hot bath infused with essential lavender oils, and she swallowed the smoothness of the hot cocoa. For a long second, she honestly considered letting Jake inside further than only her home. With both hands full, she blotted her mouth on the shoulder of her robe. "I'm perfectly honest."

"About some things, I'm sure." Jake fingered the plastic seal on the coffee pot. "You want to tell me why you're tossing a pot that's never been unveiled?" He sipped the coffee and stared at the machine in her arms.

As if she had already drunk the steaming cocoa, she felt her tummy warm until her face flushed. Why would a man like Jake have any interest in a nurse from a drive-by coastal town? Could he be strong enough to stand up to The Curse? Though she didn't want to put too much hope on the future, she unwittingly pictured an impending wedding day celebration and *her* unveiling.

Happy. Free. That was her dream.

"Whatever you're smiling about, I want to be part of that, Faith." With a single hand, he eased the clumsy pot from her arms and coiled the cord around the base. "Whatever is broken, I'll try to fix—"

"No." When he leaned forward, barely breaching the threshold by inches, to stop his forward progression, she placed her free hand on his chest. Against her palm, she felt the steady drum of his heart tempting her to inch closer and inhale the scent of a sexy man. A good man. "You'd be a fool to waste your time on this model. It's never going to be right."

"One man's castoff is another's treasure. I'm a treasure-seeker." Stepping up so his body filled the doorway, Jake loomed. "Join me."

She leaned against the heat of his thigh. He was in a higher position of power both on her step and at work, but to move forward she discarded her worries. More than anything, she wanted to be treasured. Her gown arched over his jeans. "You sure about riding together?"

"Yes. And something about this weekend with you *feels* right."

A subtle moan escaped her. Strength emanated from him. His will, as she'd witnessed during surgery, was inescapable, and to be a neurosurgeon he had to be brave. Braver than she could ever be. But, could he learn to truly trust what he couldn't see? Spirits who would continue to appear and attempt to aid him when she wasn't there to intercede? "You're a man of science…"

"What if I am? Does that solely define me?"

Whether she was a nurse, a woman from a foggy coastal town, or something else all together, she had many facets. He held her stare like he was waiting for an answer that she could not explain. Finally, she said, "You can be many things, but some aren't as desirable as the others. What if, after you've spent precious hours— hours you'll never get back—you grow tired and toss away what never had a chance?" Her vision blurred and she turned away. *Pull it together. You deserve to be happy and to find love again.*

Shifting the pot and the cup he held, he set them both on the hand-carved oak floor. He took her cup, too, and repeated his action. Then, with a gentle hand, he turned her chin, so she faced him again. "I'm asking a lot from both of us." His gaze darted to the side. "What I'm doing, saying, is completely out of character. But, I need to know you, Faith." His thumb stroked her cheek. When she swallowed, he lowered his gaze to her throat. "I'd like you to know me, but I can't do that unless you let me in."

At the sound of his uninhibited sincerity, Faith felt pleasurable warmth shoot through her that quickly changed to trembling fear. Lingering deep inside her heart that fear sat, weighted like a pending storm. The Curse…she had no control over it. He could become blind, or worse.

Live, Faith, live…

She exhaled in a great whoosh, pictured the future successful Couples Encounter, and building trust with Jake. "How much do you know about zip lining?"

"Ropes, pulleys, and carabineers. Nothing to it." With the back of his hand, he brushed a strand of hair from her eyes and flashed a reassuring smile. "Faith, you told me to follow my intuition."

Tentatively, she asked, "And it's telling you?"

"To trust you."

Before she could protest, tell him he was making a huge mistake, his thick arm curled around the small of her back and forced a gasp from her throat. Clenched by his embrace, she felt every curve of his rock-hard body through her gown, his heaving chest, their hearts pounding against each other's, as synchronized as the sounding surf that echoed in the distance. "You know nothing about me."

"We have a few hours before we're due at the retreat. While you get ready, how about you tell me everything in your life that's important to you? Everything I've missed?"

Important to me? She scrunched her brows and stared. "Who are you? Where are you from?"

"Still trying to figure out who I am. But, something tells me you're the one to show me the way home."

With his sweet breath rolling across her face, she raised on tip-toes and palmed his face. Did she dare imagine he could lead *her* heart home? "Walk away."

He lowered his face where his lips met hers.

The smooth stroke of his tongue swirled sweet cream, chocolate, and Arabica roast to create the perfect blend.

Against her lips, he breathed, "I'm not a walkaway Joe. Ever."

There, at the brink of entry into her home and heart, he stole her breath and her excuse for keeping him at bay. "Café mocha," she breathed and leaned into their first kiss. *Mercy help us both.*

FOUR

A FEW HOURS LATER, Jake pulled to a stand on top of the first zip line platform with the tree tops at eye level. He blew out a cleansing breath, but the buzz of emotions inside him had nothing to do with physical exertion from climbing the thirty-foot spiral staircase or heights. Faith's kiss lingered on his lips, her touch on his face, and stories of her childhood in Whisper Cove. Still, he knew she held back—and understood personal boundaries acutely. With a curious gaze, he watched her thread her hour-glass shape into the harness, wished his hands were the bindings that held her tight. When he noticed she'd put the specially-designed two-piece harness on upside down, he held back a chuckle.

However, like the start of a new relationship, zip lining was an extreme sport, dangerous, and stirred his protective nature both over himself and over Faith. He stepped toward her, mindful of her efforts, and righted her harness. "You sure you still want to do this?"

She glanced up, her face flushed, and scanned the other couples. "I need to do this, Jake. I may just have to ask you to push me over the edge."

No way would he do something that later she'd be pissed at him about. He couldn't wreck the partnership he was trying to build. "Faith, I'd never—"

"Jake Mitchell?" A twenty-something-year-old guide came forward with a clipboard in hand. "Your liability release sheet says you've worked as a guide and are ACCT accredited?" The guy was decked out like he owned a sportsmen's outfitters shop.

Jake's mouth tipped upward at the memory of his passion for zip lining. "Yes, back in my hometown near Las Vegas. Years ago now, but I still keep my accreditation up to date."

Giving a firm nod, the guide scribbled a note onto the page. "Fine, I'll send you out first."

Nudging his side, Faith came to stand between them with her thumbs hooked inside her shoulder harness like she wore suspenders.

"I want to go first."

Worry burrowed through him and his stomach rolled. Even though she was a capable woman, something about her going first felt wrong. But in no way did he want to insult her abilities, even as a newbie. He thrust his chin at the guide. "When was the line last checked?"

"This morning. Checked the course myself. All's good." The guide gave a thumbs-up gesture and flashed his white teeth.

But the satisfied expression on the guy's face didn't ease Jake's nerves a bit. "As a precaution—"

"Jake." Firmly, Faith's hand landed on his arm. "You've already reviewed the course's certification, maintenance, and accident records. I'll be fine."

Even though she squeezed, he could feel her shaking. He met her gaze square on and pulled her aside. Would she do something she wasn't comfortable with just to prove her strength? "Be honest with yourself. You can still back out. I won't judge you if zip lining isn't your thing."

"My stomach is doing cartwheels." Running a hand up and down Jake's arm, Faith curled her lips into a smile. "But it feels good." She popped her shoulders. "The quicker we finish, the sooner you can return to Whisper Cove and satisfy Chief Vizcaino's requirements."

His heart and breath surged, but her mention of work left him cold—reminding him of his patients' undiagnosed symptoms. He was excited to connect with Faith on a deeper level, and prove he was a man she could trust. But in turn, he needed to trust her instincts. "Alright."

Her eyes glistened for a second then, vigorously, she nodded. "Great."

However, instead of the constriction at his chest loosening, suddenly that pressure increased at having her far from him. He swallowed several times and rolled his shoulders in an attempt to work out the unwarranted kinks.

"You alright?" She cocked her head.

Was he? "I'm just trying to read you. You seem excited, scared, and sad all rolled into one."

She pumped her shoulders once. "I need this, that's all—a craving of something more, like dancing." She twirled one of the loose straps as she spun to the edge of the platform. There, she peered below to the forest ground. "The view is beautiful from up here...I can see an entire patch of blue irises. I want to purchase a few bulbs from the gift store and take them back to the laboratory for study." She glanced over her shoulder. Suddenly, her arms jerked forward and her knees wobbled like she'd completely lost her balance.

Adrenaline plowed through Jake's muscles and he lunged forward, reached for her harness where it crisscrossed her waist, and pulled her toward him. Quickly engulfing her against his abs, he experienced a sharp pang of fear—

She shoved him hard, disapproval clear by the downturned brows. "What are you doing?" she snapped.

Completely caught off-guard, he pulled back. "Saving you?"

She rolled her eyes. "I was attempting the moonwalk. I've never been so high."

"Sorry." He expelled the breath he held and, damn, if he didn't laugh outright. "We need to work on your groove, babe."

"I *was* working it." She gave him a pouty face and swiveled her hips, the rhinestones on her pants back pockets catching the diamond light.

He scrubbed his face. *What the mind witnessed didn't always make sense.* He needed to remember that and focus on building a stronger relationship within himself. "I'm not usually this protective. There's something about you…"

"I can take care of myself, but thank you." Her gaze darted to where the guide waved his arms and the half-dozen other couples lowered their voices to a low hum.

"Can I have your attention?" The guide checked his chart. "First to go, line up."

Stiffening, Jake closed the distance between him and Faith, tightened the straps around both of her legs, her chest, and pulled her closer. Something was happening between them—his emotions truly hovering on the brink where the feelings she'd awakened zinged with rawness he'd exposed without realizing.

Normally, he kept his feelings checked. But the thought of her distancing herself ratcheted up his anxiety even more. He shivered, his fear of loving and losing worn right there on his sleeve for her to see. "You first." He smiled, turned, but the touch of her fingers on his arm brought him back around.

"Wait. I've changed my mind."

He pulled back and his brows lowered as he studied the conviction in her clear eyes. In her firm words. "A moment ago you were determined to go first. Why the change?"

Exhaling, she adjusted her hair. "Because, truthfully, the ride doesn't scare me. Well, not that much. But, I'd enjoy it more knowing you were waiting at the end to catch me."

At hearing her declaration, he smiled. "You can count on me."

She blinked up at him.

Suddenly aware of the openness trapped in her wide-eyed gaze, he gave a reassuring nod. Once on the ride, you couldn't disembark. You had to endure the entire length alone, whether exhilarated or terrified. Each person's experience was unique, with no one to witness what couldn't be seen except by the birds and trees. He kissed her forehead, that sweet skin a delight against his lips, then moved to the platform where the guide readied the tether. As Jake hovered, about to push off, he realized everyone had secrets. Maybe knowing hers wasn't as important as having her believe in him as a man. "I'll be waiting."

"I'm right behind you…" she called out.

He shoved off into the abyss and held on to the image of her sky-blue eyes keeping him grounded. Pine and salt-filled air pushed against his face, up his nose, and into his mouth. As long as he could, he held her image at the forefront of his mind until speed and a green blur enveloped him fully—

A branch up ahead hung over the cable, blocking his progress, and he squeezed the brake. He came to a lurching stop and took only a moment to untangle the deadwood that must have fallen from the canopy above that he let tumble to the ground below. He released the brake and sailed toward the platform, all the while cursing himself for not standing up and voicing his internal warning. What if Faith had insisted she go first? Would she have spotted the branch and stopped in time?

Still shaken, he exited the canopy and the landing spot came into sight. A moment later, he flew onto the platform, his feet swinging up from the force. "There was a branch on the line. Someone could have gotten hurt."

The guide eyed him up and down. "Are you okay?"

"Fine. But I suggest you get someone to check all the runs."

Taking him seriously, the guide radioed ahead just as the line sang, and Faith came into view.

His heart pounded until his throat tightened. Without someone special to look forward to—rushing in, ripping him from his thoughts and forcing him to embrace new ideas—life was, frankly, not worth a damn. He exhaled long and slow. Her zip line practically sizzled as she sailed toward him.

She laughed, one hand held out, one on the brake above, her legs crossed and jutting forward just like she was an expert.

Smiling, Jake glanced toward the guide then chuckled as a buzz of warmth spread throughout his chest and nestled against his ribs. "We're going to make a great team."

The guide elbowed Jake. "Thing to remember is there are highs and lows and places between where you've got to pause and work things out. The presentation at tonight's bonfire is titled Uncovering Secrets From Within."

A sinking feeling replaced the rapture inside his chest, and he palmed the ring that lay deep in his pocket. What if, during tonight's talk, Faith saw through his stone façade and discovered the casing was actually made of glass? What if she walked away from him like Lexi had? He'd grown attached to Faith in such a short time, and he couldn't explain it rationally. But the thought of losing her…he stiffened and adjusted his harness. Though they were here to improve their *working* relationship, for Faith, he'd risk getting his heart broken again. "Talk sounds enlightening."

At the edge of the platform, ready for Faith's impending arrival, the guide said, "Falling in love is easy. Trust"—he shrugged—"a struggle, at best. Actions are based on fear both real and imagined. The secret to surviving, to living, is knowing which to believe."

Jake studied the young man. "You're quite the philosopher."

The guide scratched his head. "I can't take credit for that, but the speaker tonight will. You'll be amazed at what you can learn about yourself in only an hour."

Faith's pending landing momentarily snapped Jake's attention to her. He nudged the guide, who allowed him to catch Faith, knowing once he caught her, his life would be forever changed.

Freed from the constraints, she tossed her arms around Jake's neck and hugged him like she'd never let go. Then she did, and practically trotted toward the ladder that would take them to the platform above. "I did it. Jake, I flew so fast." She spun a pirouette like a opera house ballerina. "And here you are, waiting. I don't ever want to look back."

Neither did he.

Up ahead, where the bonfire roared, Faith stared at the assembly of couples, guides, and a lone microphone. Even though her day with Jake warmed her still, with each step leading her deeper into the belly of secrets and truths, she endured a threatening weight that steadily grew within her body. However, she held her head high and resisted giving in to fear. "Today was amazing. I wish every day could be like today." Her casual pace slowed at the spot where the irises grew unconfined, several patches having broken away from the thick clump to bridge uncharted ground.

"It was…" Jake took her hand. "It was amazing, indeed, watching you embrace something so terrifying. You're a strong woman, Faith."

She smiled up at him then movement caught her attention.

Inside the bonfire amphitheater, one of the guides had already begun to address the other couples about the night's activities. She sat on the wooden bleachers, and Jake took a seat beside her. Her insides were as jittery as the crackle that popped from the flames, and she let the image of them as a couple, once again, fill her mind. She could practically hear the sound of the church bell tolling to their uncursed union. That marriage would prove she'd passed the test, however vague the rules of that curse seemed to be. She sighed at the vision of freedom to love without conditions. Unexpectedly, a giggle escaped her throat.

Jake glanced her way. His lips curled to form a satisfied grin, and he stroked her thigh, stopping often to draw little circles on her jeans.

Was his touch from a similar thought? Could he also feel the attraction between them, the trust building? Drawn to his touch, she scooted closer, inhaling his spiced cologne tinged with the scent of forest and campfire. "We had quite a day. No telling what tonight will bring…"

"We did." He lifted his arm to yoke her shoulder and pulled her close. "This is nice."

Even though his voice's heady tone made her belly warm even more, the weight of his arm trapped her to the truth. If she didn't open her world to him, she'd never be free of The Curse. "Almost perfect."

Almost. She had faced her fear every time she leaped from each platform. Every time she sought out the landing, she had found him waiting with arms wide. Sharing her ability to speak to the dead was forbidden, but what if, secretly, that's what needed to be risked to break The Curse? Taking a leap, what if she shared what she knew of the Lover's Curse—a baby step—would he be the kind of man who would stay? Inhaling, she let her breath leach out. "Jake, I have something to tell you—"

"Can I have your attention?" The guide spoke into the microphone ten feet away. He held an acoustic guitar in his hands. "Our program will start in a few minutes. Let's begin with a love song…" He strummed a few bars to "Baby I'm A Want You" by Bread.

Leaning close, mouth at her ear, Jake asked,

"What were you going to say?"

Jake, I'm cursed. Loving me will put you in danger. Changing your mind about loving me can be deadly. Run. She swallowed against her dry throat, splintered like the stacked firewood. "There's a legend in Whisper Cove—"

The thud of the microphone nearly popped Faith off her seat, and a screech snapped her attention front and center to the man standing there holding his red-tipped white cane at his side. The man had dark brown eyes, short hair, a dark pea coat over khaki pants...

How could this be?

She froze, her stare flashing wide, so the campfire smoke burned until her eyes teared. At least she blamed her watering eyes on the smoky irritant. Blinking, she tried desperately to ease the sting.

Jake's grip on her arm, him shaking her, barely registered. The fire blurred, but the introduction of Steven Silva, her ex-fiancé, blared like the microphone volume had risen tenfold.

Steven barely filled out the clothes that once hugged his muscular body. His dirty blond hair was no longer cut in a professional style but a buzz cut. Simple.

Ruined. The night was ruined.

The Curse upon her.

"Say something. Faith?"

She blinked and attempted to answer Jake. Then she stood and took a wobbly step. She wasn't ready to *show* Jake the damage caused by her secret. "Oh, God. Steven—"

"Faith? Is that you?" Steven tapped his cane on the sandy ground and took several unsteady steps before coming to stand only an arm's length away. "What are you doing here?"

Jake swiveled his head to face the speaker, his gaze darting between her and Steven. Jake pushed to standing then sank a hand inside his pocket. "You know each other?"

Even though he was blind, Steven glared in Jake's direction. "Yes. Has Faith not mentioned her darkest secret?"

The whites of Jake's eyes flashed. "What we've shared is none of your business." He held Faith's gaze as he spoke and took her hand in his.

Trembling, even on the inside, she mouthed, "Thank you." But how did she catch her breath? Now, how did she convince herself to prove to

Jake she wasn't worth fixing when she felt complete with him by her side? Gathering her might, she dragged her foot backward and felt the support in her knees give way, only to be replaced by the consistency of jelly.

Jake caught her arm, holding her tight. "Let's sit…"

"Yes," she mumbled and felt the back of his hand on her forehead. Was he checking her temperature? After all day in the sun, she hadn't considered heat exhaustion could claim her energy. But, who was she fooling? The Curse had her in its sights again. And Jake would never give up on her. He was that kind of man. He was protective and willing to endure hardships Steven had run from.

She needed to be more like Jake. Ask questions. Make decisions based on facts in lieu of feelings.

Only tomorrow was another day where she'd have to return home. Cutting emotional ties with Jake was the right thing to do. "I'm okay. Really. Just surprised to see Steven."

Steven removed his glasses, his stare shooting past her to somewhere in the distance. "I'm the one who's surprised." *You've moved on so quickly.*

Two years since he'd left her, and Steven's unspoken words lay in his condemning gaze. "I've decided to move ahead with my life."

He twisted his head.

She shuddered from the confliction brewing between Steven's stare and her guilt at having caused his blindness—though he'd left her. She flicked her gaze to Jake, only to meet his darkened hazel eyes laced with questions she wasn't ready to answer or deny.

Jake had kissed her repeatedly, showing he had feelings for her.

She wasn't so blind she did not see the credence in his eyes of a man who intended to claim his woman, nor could she not feel the passion in his grip on her arm. But, seeing Steven reminded her of the damage that could happen if Jake professed his commitment then changed his mind about loving her. She'd acted foolishly today, putting Jake in danger. She couldn't make that mistake again.

The microphone squealed. "Coffee, hot chocolate, and cider are available. In a few moments, we'll start the program." Several people headed in the direction of the coffee station set up near the stack of firewood, the firelight casting long shadows into the night, and a few curious couples held the three of them with lingering stares.

Steven took another step toward her, so his cane rested against her leather boot. "You haven't returned any of my calls." He turned his head to where Jake stood, his gaze at Jake's chest level. "Now I know why." He held out his hand toward Jake. "I'm Steven Silva. Life coach."

Jake eyed Steven's hand a moment before grasping it. "Dr. Jake Mitchell. Neurologist at Full Sail. Faith and I—"

"Work together," she finished.

Soon as her words rushed out, shadows accumulated in Jake's eyes.

Two words had reduced their budding relationship to colleagues, but she knew her word choice was for Jake's safety. A pain shot straight through her chest, and she placed her hand over her heart. The Curse demanded sacrifice, truth, and unconditional love. If she didn't elevate her desire to move forward with her life above her fear, she'd never be free of The Curse.

Jake's brows lifted. "So, how long have you

been a life coach?"

"For almost two years." Steven cleared his throat. "Right now, I'm picking up from each of you a hint of more than a working relationship."

Holding her stare, Jake's jaw rocked, but she turned away. Heart pounding, she glanced over her shoulder to the cottage each couple was supposed to spend the night in, housed somewhere deep in the shadowed forest. All along she'd been asking Jake to believe in a feeling and to consider that intuition the key to saving his life.

But, Jake had responded in a way she hadn't expected. He made their connection personal. He'd put his faith in her. Deeper than she could have hoped for. Again, she'd pushed aside a worthy man because of her fear of hurting him. Maybe encouraging Steven to fulfill his dreams of becoming a renowned composer without her at his side had caused him to choose to leave her? Maybe through her actions he believed she hadn't loved him? Made sense. Perfect sense. In retrospect, her feelings toward Steven hadn't spanned half the distance she already felt for Jake. And that made little sense. "I'm still challenging hope that something more will become of our partnership."

"To benefit our working environment," Jake appended.

By Jake's flat expression and his hands tucked inside his pockets, she'd hurt him more than she could know. "Some challenges are harder than others. But, I'm willing to face my fears. Willing to go deeper than I've ever gone." She pinned her gaze on Jake's until he glanced away.

Steven buttoned up his jacket. "Well, let me not come between your—coupling." At the sound of the microphone tuning, he stiffened.

Behind him, others sat waiting for him to begin.

Raking his hair, Jake divided the silky waves into furrows and stared at Steven, his eyes narrowing. "So, how do you two know each other?"

"I'm the dreaded ex-fiancé who left her groomless on our wedding day."

Gaping, Jake split his gaze between the two. "Steven Silva is your ex? The guy that left you standing at the altar is our speaker on trust? Now that's a speech I'm interested in hearing."

Disapproving murmurs from the other

couples heightened to outright protests. Several burst to standing.

To answer Jake's question, she nodded slowly then turned to leave, but Jake reached out and held her shoulder. Suddenly, the heat of his body was pressed against her back and his hot breath raced up her neck.

"Faith, don't go. Let's face this together. Let's…trust each other. Isn't that why we're here?"

The purr of his voice reached out and caressed her spine, but she tucked her elbows to her sides. "Yes, but I'm cursed."

"You can't believe that. I don't."

At his resolute statement, gently, she tugged away. Not having the capacity to stare him in the eyes, she faced the direction of the cabin and spoke into the breeze. "As hard to believe as Tori knowing her life was in danger? As unbelievable as a wedding day breakup that caused the ex-groom's blindness? As unlikely as a branch on a wire? Yes, I heard the guides talking about how you saved the day."

"What?" His voice was soft and gentle. "Faith…please, look at me…."

"I-I can't do this." Before tears could stream

down her face, she focused on her even steps and headed toward the cottage they were supposed to spend the night sharing. She kept her head held high, knowing damn well she'd betrayed her own heart by letting her fear of again losing come between her and Jake. Sadly, instead of Jake, she'd been the one to run away, and that had nothing to do with being cursed.

$\mathfrak{F}$IVE

"LET HER GO," Steven said in a commanding tone.

"Back off." Jake balled his fists. Last thing he wanted was to listen to Faith's ex give him advice about the woman his heart pined for. His gaze followed her silhouette into the misty darkness, and he could tell by her steady pace and upright posture that she, once again, didn't need him. His stomach twisted all the way into his throat. He wished for her to turn and invite him to walk that thin path with her, but she never did. Chest aching, he spun around. Maybe talking to Steven about Faith was the fastest way to understand why she kept rejecting him? "You don't know anything about us," he whispered.

"I only wish I had let her go sooner…"

To get a better look at Steven's expression, Jake held up his hand and blocked the fire's roaring glare. At the certainty stark in Steven's dark brown eyes, Jake stiffened. "Maybe she wasn't right for you."

Steven scoffed. "I suppose, in hindsight, everything is clear. Easy. But then, Faith made everything easy. That was her lure."

To Jake, ease wasn't his lure, though she did evoke a peace-filled feeling inside him, one of comfort and home. "We see her in a different light."

"Perhaps that is why my sight was taken the day I decided to spare her from the Lover's Curse."

"Lover's Curse?" He jerked his head in Steven's direction, a deep chill washing over him he couldn't warm no matter how tight he wrapped his jacket around his torso. "Faith believes she's afflicted. I've heard rumors about the town. But this talk of a curse isn't real."

"I wish that were true." Tapping his cane on the smooth earth, Steven came to stand directly in front of Jake. He tossed his head toward the empty amphitheater that Jake's comment had caused. "Since I no longer have an audience, how about I tell you what you need to hear?"

Though every muscle in his body wanted to

reject the notion of turning his attention from Faith to Steven, he had to discover why she kept pushing him away. Pinching his gaze, he zeroed his focus in on the cane. "We can talk closer to the fire. Coffee?"

"We can start there." Steven held out his arm. "Do you mind?"

After a trip to the coffee kiosk, the fire crackling, Jake sat beside Steven in the front row. Heat from the fire crawled up Jake's calves, and he sipped his coffee, letting the bitter-tasting heat soothe away the chill that worked through his bones. "I'm listening."

Cupping his drink, Steven took a slurpy sip, steam coiling into the air. "A belief in something beyond facts can't be easy for you. You're a man of medicine…"

Even though Jake's inside voice was telling him to conceivably see the world in shades of grey, he answered in a firm tone, "Most legends can be disproved through scientific means."

"Most. As a doctor, I'm sure you've paid a visit to the morgue…felt the cold chill and unease quicken your pace, an inexplicable static charge during a touch-and-go surgery, perchance heard your name carried on a breeze, or spied a shadow that moved but, when you sought it out, stilled."

Chills vibrated down his spine. He clenched his fists to keep them from visibly shaking. "Imagination runs wild from viewing too many late-night horror films."

"No." Steven shook his head, staring right at him. Through him. "It's intuition. Intuition your life depends on if you're to survive The Curse unscathed."

At the weight of each word, Jake pulled back and studied Steven's serious glare. Though a shiver quaked through him, he leaned forward and rested his elbows on his knees. "She's special, but I'm not sure she's into me."

Steven looked his way and sat taller. "Since I lost my sight, my remaining senses have sharpened. Faith's voice trembled, and the brush of her jacket raked against her sides as she marched off. She's afraid I'll tell you about The Curse. It's the one thing she shared with me—"

"Such things aren't real…" Jake let his sentence fall. Staring into the fire, he thought about when he'd returned home from the hospital and tried to close his eyes only to see Faith's face, her beautiful face, but also something more: her discomfort in having to work with him. Then he'd had the dream…one moment of ecstasy when he'd slipped the ring he carried onto Faith's finger, the next, he rolled the ring between his thumb and forefinger and tried to make out the fuzzy image of a woman in a hospital bed who lay unconscious and breathing from a ventilator. He shook at the nightmare's vision and visibly shivered.

That's why he'd gone to the hospital to check on Tori, only to find her squeezing her husband's hand. Then he'd sought out Patti and convinced her he needed Faith's address STAT. Patti had proceeded to recommend he take Faith a loaded cup of coffee but suggested giving her another option—if he actually wanted to get farther than the porch.

"Ah…back to that." Steven retrieved a scarf from his jacket pocket and single-handedly looped the flannel material around his neck. "Have any of your patients complained of headaches?" He leaned closer. "Heard voices?"

Jake snapped his attention to Steven so quickly a pain shot through his neck. "Go on…tell me what you know."

"You'll find those patients are not Founding

Family members. They are outsiders. Like I once was. Like you are."

Stretching upward, Jake took a mouthful of coffee and swallowed. He had yet to be afflicted with head pain. All his life, he'd been an outsider looking to make connections as a way to feel safe. But, he glared at the man who knew too much about the sleepy town. "I'm sure there's something in the environment triggering the phenomenon."

"Like I said…a Lover's Curse." A breath later, Steven asked, "Do you love Faith?"

Spewing his coffee, he cupped his mouth, coughing. "Do you think you're some kind of shrink? That I need therapy? Well, think again."

Did he love Faith? Could he, when he'd only met her two days prior? However, that moment he'd seen her in the hallway standing with the chief, she'd stirred something primal within him, a sixth sense…after spending today together, he realized how fast he'd grown to care for her. He pictured her inside the cabin where he couldn't comfort her, which made his chest clench, beginning deep inside right where his heart lay. A place that had never been touched by anyone so deeply, not even Lexi. And more, his protectiveness raged, as did the thought of building a life with Faith, no matter how many secrets she carried. In spite of her beliefs, fact or fiction, he was definitely falling for her.

Maybe even loved her, if that were possible.

Quickly, he corralled his emotions. "It's getting late."

"Yes, darkness is upon you now, but stay. Please, stay." Steven took another long gulp. "Let me explain...I *loved* music. Composing was my life. My love—"

"Composing?" He eyed the cane.

"Before The Curse...before I lost my sight, I composed for the San Francisco Opera. Then I met Faith at a little coffee shop on Market Street. I should have been honest with my feelings from the beginning. But, I wasn't. In the end"—he chugged the remainder of his coffee and wiped his mouth on his scarf—"I did indeed leave her, but sadly, she blames herself for my misfortune."

"Misfortune?" His brows jumped up and his coffee sloshed out the cup's lip and dribbled across his thumb. He'd seen her dance today. He wanted her to dance again, to open up instead of run away. "What do you mean by that?"

"The day I left Faith, our wedding day, I lost what I truly loved." Crumpling the cup, Steven exhaled. He placed the squashed cup on the bench beside him. "Without the composer, the opera does not exist. Nor vice versa."

"So, you *did* love her." Jake set his cooled cup down and massaged his head, noticing Steven twist in the direction Faith had gone. Maybe it was better Jake and Faith parted now. Faith obviously had unfinished business with this guy. But, the thought that she could still love Steven made his stomach turn. "If you loved her, and she you, if she was willing to risk her life, and you yours"—though Jake still wasn't convinced a curse existed or that he could truly move past his feelings toward Faith, he added—"you should tell her."

"No..." Steven tapped his cane and stood. He angled his feet toward the cabin. "You might think me a monster, but I'm not. I was only honest with myself...however, too late, and wanted more for her. More than me traveling the world and being gone for months at a time, leaving her behind. I wanted to see her happy. I still do."

A quiver of indecision ripped through him.

He speared his hair, thinking what the hell he was doing dishing on the woman of his dreams when he needed to fight for her. All his life, those he'd loved had been taken from him. His mother. His aunt. His say in those matters had held little weight. Yet, there was a pattern that suddenly emerged. Every time he'd silenced his gut feeling, he'd been reprimanded by pain and loss. In his ex's, aunt's, and Tori's cases, he'd let them down by not backing his feelings with actions. He no longer wanted to repeat that pattern. "I'm going to be there for Faith. No matter what. All your talk of omens is not enough to scare me away."

Sneering, Steven lifted his chin. "You misunderstand. And this is what you need to realize. I *loved* the opera. That's what The Curse stole from me, what I loved, and that was not Faith. I'm to live for the rest of my life blind. The life I imagined is destroyed. But Faith,"—he half-smiled and added a clucking sound—"she deserves someone like you."

At the negative tone, Jake pushed to standing. He darted his gaze to the glow emanating from their cottage porch—a beacon that led him to Faith. "I'm going out on a limb.

I'm not your neurologist or psychiatrist, but your symptoms are most likely caused by emotional trauma and are guilt induced." Jake patted his wallet, certain inside lay a card from a specialist who owed him a favor. "I'm sure there's a good medical explanation for your condition, if you're willing to have an open mind."

"And vice versa. Because what will you lose, Dr. Mitchell? How will you perform surgeries without your hands, your mind?"

What is this guy talking about? Jake inhaled then held that breath, contemplating his answer.

"Perhaps you'll be one of the lucky few who survive The Curse." Steven tightened his scarf, stood, and popped up his jacket's collar. He bent down, retrieved the discarded cup, and shoved it in his pocket. "But, let me ask you…if you love Faith, are you ready to see misfortune, even death, bestowed upon her?"

Might as well have been a sledgehammer that socked him in the gut. *No, higher.* Right over his heart. Like that nightmare, the thought of Faith in pain sent him reeling backward. Someplace inside him he avoided, someplace hidden that suddenly burst, made his answer hover on the tip of his tongue. Yes—with every molecule that made up the latticework of his being and the spaces between, more in-depth than what could be defined through scientific means—he sensed a change as his feelings for Faith amplified.

"Good day…" Steven waved a hand. "I mean, goodnight."

"Hold up…" Jake searched his wallet, pulled out the card, pushed it into Steven's hand, and wrapped the guy's fingers around the embossed lettering. "On this card is the name of an excellent specialist. Maybe *you'll* get lucky."

"You don't believe in luck, Doctor." Steven fingered the card then walked in the direction of where the other couples congregated, their distant singing rising into the night air.

Without hesitation, Jake strode toward the cabin where mist gathered at his feet and rose up in his wake. He shivered, lifted his cell from his pocket, and punched in the only number at Full Sail he knew by heart. When the chief's voice mail kicked in, Jake spoke in terse sentences. "Chief. This is Dr. Mitchell. I'm taking a stand here, yes, risking passing probation, but if you have faith in me and my skills, I'm the one who decides who I work with. If Faith prefers pediatrics, I want her transferred back, if she verifies that decision. For the good of the hospital, I hope you see that a person's feelings at times outweigh facts, and protocol."

He ended the call and felt a weight lift from his shoulders, his pace quickening even more. Whether he'd have a job to return to come Monday morning, he couldn't be sure, but at least he'd taken a stand. And on that narrow dirt path, fog crowding in on him, leaves crackling underfoot, he opened his mind to accepting his feelings for Faith. Now, he needed to convince her, whether cursed or not, she was loved.

INSIDE THE CABIN, Faith paced the wooden floors, her bare feet slapping the planks that complained with each step. Her tummy tightened to the point of nausea, and she swallowed past the pain-filled lump that crowded her throat. Steven should have been the cause of her turmoil. His blindness. His failing health.

Should have been. Instead, her mind was locked on Jake's downturned eyes and the fact he had tried to stop her from leaving when she shouldn't have left in the first place.

Hugging herself, she had a sudden realization the flame Jake had ignited inside of her was in danger, not from The Curse, but from herself. Maybe, instead of running, she needed to face her fear of rejection and heartbreak head on. Learn to be loved for who she was, cursed or not, and share with Jake the re-awakened feelings she never thought would rise again. She had to let go of what she couldn't control, and simply live.

"Faith!"

Jake's voice, though distant, reached her ears, and she spun to face the screen door. He was coming…calling her name, the echo urgent.

Her insides fluttered, anxious, excited. For a minute, silently, she stood frozen. After she'd run off, was it possible he cared enough to come for her and not just to seek out his lodging for the night?

At a minimum, if he didn't reciprocate her feelings, at least she'd finally allowed herself to feel the thrumming hint that more than a friendship or partnership had found her again. She smiled until her cheeks plumped with jubilation.

Jake's cries faded…

But, she kept her heart as open as the door she now pressed wide.

Outside, stretching its branched wings into the fog-filled night sky, she should have seen death waiting within the old oak tree and within the spirit-crowded forest. The Curse summoned the ghostly silhouettes.

She should have backed away from under the weighted branches that curled over the cabin roof. That threatened to fall, to crush, and maim. And, backed away from the threatening stares of the waiting spirits.

But, though she glared at that massive tree with the leafed limbs that refused to let go of life as did the spirits, she took a step forward onto the porch. Then another, until she stood on the lowest step with the mist curling at her toes. Silently, she challenged The Curse, the misty fog that blanketed the lowland that split the cottages.

Though fear coursed through her in chilling waves, she didn't tremble.

Yes. If a healthy partnership hovered on the horizon with the goal of saving lives, she needed to start by saving her own.

Six

ON THE DARKENED cabin porch, Jake found Faith sitting on the lowest step, her feet planted in the dirt, her gaze focused on an oak tree draped in twisted, heavy branches that faded into the surrounding fog.

She didn't turn her head or gaze toward him, even as he sat beside her. "Hey, you okay?"

In slow, steady strokes, she rubbed her denim-covered knees. "Death comes in many forms…" she answered. "Even when figurative, the sting can burn."

A chill skittered down his back and his brows rolled forward, as did his body. He focused on the star-fire in her eyes and agreed. He assumed she was talking about her and Steven's split, but somehow, he felt her tone held more meaning, her injury carved deeper than what could be seen… "Moving forward doesn't have to be painful."

In profile, her cheek crimped from her subtle smile but didn't reach her eyes. She continued to gaze at the tree. "But what if you're stuck? What if you can't break free from your beliefs for fear you'll take down whoever stands in your way?"

He stared to where she looked, to that tree's skeleton, the shadowed crook, the acute angle of the lower branch, and the trunk's slant that hung directly over the fog shrouded cabin. Sure, the branch could come crashing down at any moment, as oaks were self-shedding. However, that tree had rooted there for hundreds of years. "Sometimes, you have to do right by the tree. Let others watch out for themselves. I think you pushed me away because you're protecting me from something. A secret. A curse…"

She jerked her head toward him, eyes wide. "Steven told you."

"Yeah." He added a nod.

"Did he tell you I'm a direct descendant of a Founding Family? That a shaman cursed all descendants to a Lover's Curse? That Steven changing his mind about loving me left him blind, his dreams destroyed?"

"Yes, and I understand your aversion to coffee."

Her chest rose and fell, and she cupped her mouth. "I can't bear the memory of our last—before he—he—left me."

"Shhh…I know. It's okay." He pulled her against his chest. With his palm rubbing circles on her back, he felt her ribs bump his hand with her sobs. Symbols, whether a loved one's ring or an unused coffee pot, could stir emotions that sliced the heart and soul, that made one yearn for something more, or less. He sniffed and hoped she didn't see him wipe his eyes. "I'm guessing the pot was a wedding gift."

"Engagement." She glanced up at him, her eyes glossy. "I shouldn't be telling you these things. They've kept me stuck in the past when I want to move forward."

"Faith"—he thumbed his chest—"I'm not worried about curses, or your memories that don't include me."

She dragged her shoe across the silty earth, drawing an arch and then adding branches until she'd perfected her version of the tree. "Only a fool would put himself in harm's way for no good reason. If I can stop that, I'm obligated to try."

An inward breeze ruffled the canopy, and the resulting *crack* from somewhere deep in the trunk caused Jake to tense. Or perhaps the grip that clenched his insides was caused by Faith's distress. He reached into her lap and covered her hand, giving her a gentle squeeze that, in turn, calmed him. He chuckled at how she humbled him. How she brought him to his knees and made him gaze at her like she did that pillar with leaves.

Even in the shadows, the truth shone. Then he saw the similarity between this woman, this strong woman, and that magnificent tree, however distorted. "I *see* the tree, Faith." He leaned his shoulder against hers. "I *see* it in the shadows, hollowed out from time. Weary, splintered. Raw. And still enduring. Just like I see you."

She raised her head and met his gaze. "How can you understand me so well?"

Jake inhaled, ready to confess the answer. "Because we belong together."

Threatening to spill unshed tears, she blinked several times. "We do?"

He tucked a piece of her hair behind her ear.

"Tell me you feel it, Faith. Tell me you want to step into the future with me."

She glanced away, but with his index finger, he guided her chin so she'd look at him. "I let Chief make decisions for me. I put my instincts on the shelf many times and have seen the repercussions." The hand he held, he pressed a bit tighter. "I'm not doing that ever again. Because I choose where I stand. *Me*. I want you to choose to do the same."

She stared at her feet, adding a few more branches to the drawing. "At any moment, when you least expect it, a branch could come crashing down. That's what uncertainty of our future would hold." She faced him. "You could be trapped, injured, maybe even die. You could suffer The Curse like—"

And there it was…the darkness that flashed in her eyes, the concern and lies she believed that, if he chanced loving her, he'd be embedded in disaster. While his mind was still lost in saving her from her doubts and showing he loved her, he slid one arm around her back, the other under her knees, and pulled her into his lap. "You deserve to be happy. We both do. If there's a risk in loving you, then I'll gladly accept that."

Those blue eyes stared up at him. From the cabin's light spilling outside, he saw her gaze was more beautiful than any nightscape.

She glanced away. "Then you're a fool."

His mouth curved upward. "What if I am? What If I called Chief Vizcaino and demanded he reinstate your position in pediatrics? What if I set my own limits on who I work with?"

She gasped. "Oh, Jake... What if you don't pass probation?"

He shrugged then lifted his hands to palm her flushed cheeks. He smoothed away her tears. "I can't control the future. Only this moment."

To match hers, he parted his lips. He placed his forehead against hers, so she would not be distracted by the tree or the far-off bonfire's glow through the mist. "For someone I love, I'd risk being crushed. For someone I love, I'd risk my life and die right along with them. Because, Faith Cabrillo, you make me want to be your hero. I'll never second guess that. I could question why, but the feeling simply exists, and it feels damn good when I'm with you."

A gust shook the canopy, and the wind whistled through the fog that thinned. Several twigs trickled to the forest floor and landed with a snap.

"For you, Faith, I'd stop that tree from falling—no matter what."

"Oh, Jake."

Her lips quivered then met his, an urgent kiss when he'd expected a soft one. With the distant fire's amber glow lighting the forest so the trees' shadows seemed like an audience, he closed his eyes and enveloped her, drank her down but couldn't be quenched.

"Coffee," she whispered against his mouth. "I want to make coffee with you…."

He smiled wide, because he'd broken through her barrier. He lifted her, stormed through the cabin door, and bypassed the couch he'd intended to sleep on. "Mmmm, we'll make beautiful coffee together, Faith. Trust me on that. Coffee you'll crave for a lifetime…I'll make sure of that."

THE PILLOW-TOP MATTRESS was not as luxurious as Jake's lips that meandered down Faith's neck, along her shoulder, and lower, like fallen stars that sprinkled her skin in searing kisses. As if he read her mind, he slid his hands up inside her blouse, lifted the shirt in one slow tug, and unsnapped her bra to expose her aching breasts.

Hands exploring, tongue trailing, Jake used his warm fingers to twist and pluck her breasts until the pebbles tightened with sensation.

She arched into him and threaded her fingers through his thick hair and, with her thumbs, traced the outline of his ears—perfect ears, both firm and soft. With her moans, and by the sway of her hips, she encouraged his discovery. Captured by the freefall, the exhilaration, the passion, how could loving Jake—yes, loving him—be wrong? "Jake…"

He pulled away for a fretful minute, and the cool air that replaced his warmth caused her breath to hitch. Then he was on her, his bare chest against hers, his weight filling her need that was growing to a vast and ever-increasing expanse. Simultaneously, their breaths combined until she began to writhe beneath him.

"I'll make you feel so good, Faith, you'll never want to leave this cabin."

A heat wave flashed over her body, and she tugged him down, his mouth and hips tormenting her without giving her what she really wanted. Him inside her so deep, so thoroughly buried, that, indeed, he could not leave her if he tried. She sucked in a breath, shared the air between them, and the decadent groans that emanated from deep within him became a constant she clung to.

He slid his hand to her waistband, skimming the denim, begging entry without words.

Undulating against his hand's pressure, her breath caught. With a tug, her jeans fell to the floor.

"Beautiful...you're so beautiful, Faith."

His once-even voice became a ragged, pain-filled sound—the way a man holds inside his desire to both satisfy and be satisfied.

And release, she would give him. Again and again.

Breaching her panties, he circled his fingers on the tingle-filled knot, that bud his expert coaxing inflamed. Anticipating a long stroke, she cried out, rocking desperately, wanting, bucking against the building pressure that would not cease. For he did not plan on quick release, she predicted, but pleasurable seconds that filled the entire night. "Please, Jake, I need—"

His hot kiss stole her words. But in that moment, with love stark in his eyes, she believed they had a chance to destroy The Curse. She moved his hand to her core, let him touch the wetness that burst from within…desire his touch had solely created. Ready, so ready to open herself to his wiles, she spread her legs wider, oh, wider still…

But he pressed back on his arms and those hazel eyes narrowed. The side of his mouth tipped upward.

His sense of control was either a gift or a curse, she wasn't sure. She stared into his eyes, laden with desire, and saw his jaw clenching and releasing.

With his hand on her panties, he fiddled with the little bow. "I. Want. You."

Swallowing, she understood once that barrier of cloth was removed, there would be no turning back for either of them. Maybe already they were too late. "Take me."

With a snap, that delicate lace that once spanned her hip was removed, followed by his lips on hers. Then he froze, his exhalation sizzling on her cheek.

She let out a deflating breath, both of body

and soul. Of course, he would stop. He was obviously having second thoughts—

Palms gripped her cheeks and he kissed her hard, almost to the point of pain that came to a forceful halt. "I want you. Badly…" His focus on the nightstand to the left of the headboard lowered. "I don't have any condoms…."

He wasn't prepared, and that only made her respect him more. Want him more. "I take it you weren't a Boy Scout?"

He groaned. "How I regret that decision right now."

Kissing his mouth, her lips hungry for more of what he could give her, she felt her core cry with need. She rolled to her side of the bed, shooting her best attempt at a "sexy" look over her shoulder, and yanked open the drawer. She checked the expiration date, the cool air nipping at her legs, her swollen breasts. "It's a couples retreat with full amenities. An entire box of ten." A smile bloomed that she tried to conceal with her hand.

"That's all…?" He pumped his brows and grinned.

She giggled, handed him a condom, and lay beside him once again. The silvery orb in the sky cast light through the mist-filled window that highlighted Jake's square pecs and the waves that rode his abs. "Beautiful..." she whispered. She let her hands feast on the strength his body held.

He crinkled the condom and, in a fury, bit through the gold wrapper.

With fervor, he rolled the barrier over his thick member until she could no longer resist the temptation to reach out and touch the firmness pumped so thick, so powerful. Boundless virility. She hissed a breath and began to shimmy down the length of his body—

Forceful hands gripped her shoulders and held her, just held her.

And she let him. Let the rhythm of his heart pound in her ear. Let his steadiness fill her. Let the moment extend to minutes...

"Lay back, babe," he commanded. "Let me take care of you."

"But, I want—"

"Not this first time." He rolled her onto her back, his weight pinning her to the mattress, his forearms hugging her shoulders while his fingers threaded through her hair.

The air in her chest, the blood that filled her veins, heated with desire. "I want to please you…"

"Faith, more than you know, you already have." Hungry lips met hers, the sweep of his tongue teased her mouth open.

In utter relief, she sighed and wrapped her legs around his hips, drawing him close, so that pleasurable extension of him neared the edge of no return. "Make me yours, Jake." In her mind, she added, "Make me whole."

His tender gaze met hers. He didn't glance away or blink or stammer when he said, "Promise you'll do the same."

She nodded, and in one long thrust, he pushed his length into her, rousing that bundle of nerves, that place of pleasure she'd heard existed, but had never felt flame. For hours, seemed like days, he teased, withdrew and marched forward, retreated, then plundered in a tantric rhythm that would find no end.

"Faith, you're heaven." His voice caught. "Babe, heav—"

She opened her eyes to see his head tilt back and jaw gritting his pleasure.

Her orgasm struck hard, a great flare that burst forth, as if somehow instead of him waiting for her to reach a peak, she'd been waiting for him. Pulses grabbed and propelled her to a place where thought did not exist. Only ecstasy that gained speed, height… "Oh, Jake…"

Right in time, with stars and moon low in the sky and a new day still in its infancy, together they cried out each other's names again and again. Felt the earth move, the wind whirl mist against the window pane. And in those final moments, she granted him his wish. And he did hers.

Then the night began again.

$\mathcal{S}$EVEN

WITH THE AROMA of coffee so thick and rich it hung in the air, Jake licked his lips, the sensation tingling from kissing Faith all night long. He focused his gaze on her while she sipped her dark roast, her eyes closed and satiated. Just the way he wanted to keep her…blissfully happy. "You're so gorgeous…"

She smiled and gave him a playful look that had him crawling across the kitchen table, crinkling the day's newspaper he'd been skimming, and planting his lips firmly on hers.

"You keep saying that, Jake Mitchell, and I just might believe you."

And I might have to make you mine permanently…

At the suddenness of that silent pledge, he slid back into his seat, the wooden chair feeling less firm than it had a moment before. The newspaper fell open to the obituaries, and his mind skittered back to his past. To his memory of loss and pain. Of checked feelings and facts.

A steady knock on the door startled him and he lifted his head to see Faith dart toward the door. His beautiful Faith he didn't want to associate with discomfort.

When the door cracked open, Jake breathed in the scent of the forest and all life had to offer.

The guide handed her a flyer. "Couples Encounters is offering a final zip lining session before checkout. If you want to take part, meet at the first platform in a half-hour."

After she closed the door, Faith turned and sighed. "I'd like to go once again."

Seeing her standing there in his white tee that covered her bareness, he wanted to rip off that barrier like he had her panties. Still, although hours had passed, he felt his heart throbbing though his mind was restless. How could he be man enough for her? "Didn't you get enough zip lining yesterday?"

"I'm not talking about zip lining. What do you say we make good use of that pillow-top first?"

Clearly, lack of sleep and Faith's loving arms had him imagining his life with her. Their children's faces, and so much more. But, commitment… He wanted more. So much more than a single night. A single weekend.

He wanted forever.

Though words didn't come, he let her lead him toward the bedroom while he fought to decipher the feelings inside. Didn't take her but a moment to turn that half-hour into a memory he would never forget. Then they were showered, packed, and ascending the first platform's stairway, flying from platform to platform until they reached the last course. And still, that thought of forever lingered with a sort of urgency that gripped his gut, his mind, and his heart.

Standing on the last platform 300 feet above the ravine, a river below reduced to a tiny stream, Faith insisted on going first.

But something was in her stillness, that crinkle of joy in her eyes had faded. He reached out and pulled her close. "A kiss before our last time…"

On tiptoes, she kissed him chastely, her arms hugging around his neck with a brief squeeze. "Don't worry about me…" She pulled from his arms and headed to the edge of the platform.

A chill of fear shot through him, and he stepped forward. He gripped her harness to keep her from leaving and nestled his cheek next to hers. "I'm never going to stop worrying about you…never going to stop caring."

Faith smiled, and then she shoved off.

Jake moved beside the guide, gripping the railing, watching her sail along the line without glancing back. That weighted feeling of dread washed over him again, and he staggered backward. "Something's wrong."

The guide stared at Jake and squinted. "What's going on?"

That's when something hit Jake, more than a feeling, a premonition of sorts that a tough situation was about to present itself. Something he imagined Tori had felt and followed. "She's in trouble."

"Trouble?" The guide thrust his palms to rest on his hips. "What kind of—She's using the brake mid-span…"

Telling himself to relax, Jake breathed slowly. But that was life, things didn't always fly along steadily—there were holdups, slow spots, and times when a person just froze up in panic. Jake had been affectionate and considering a long-term commitment all morning. And Faith's sensitivity had locked on to his desire. Maybe even scared her.

Relationships are complicated, he remembered one of the guides saying. Jake agreed, there were highs and lows and places between where you take pause and work things out.

"What's she doing out there? She's not supposed to stop."

"You tell me." Jake shot back.

With her legs hanging downward as she came to a stop that split the distance between where Jake stood helpless and where she needed to go, she hung her head, like she might be crying.

Jake's heart shot into his throat. "I'm going after her."

The guide thrust out his arm. "That's against policy. You have to be certified."

Jake gave a quick nod. "Check in the office for my registration number."

"You'll need to wait until I get confirmation."

"I'll be on the other side by then." Jake hooked his carabineer to the tether. "She needs me. I'm there for her." Seemed like that was his new motto, which was fine by him. He shoved off with the guide shouting threats. Next, Jake found himself sailing, flying toward Faith, the wind rushing past until he grabbed the brake and slid slowly behind her. Cautiously, he reached out and touched her shoulder. "Hey, babe…"

"Hey…" She glanced behind her, dried tears on her flushed face. "Why are you here?"

Why was he here? She didn't need to be rescued, not really. The cable wasn't crimped or hanging with debris. Certainly, she needed only to release the brake and their time at Couples Encounters would be over.

Over.

Ended. The perfect night coming to a dead stop because of the commitment he needed to profess to this woman he loved, but had skirted. "I'm sorry."

"There's nothing for you to be sorry about. Soon as I let go, two minutes tops from right now, and we can go back to real life. It's better that way. Really…"

He shuddered, and the tether that held him rocked. "That's not an option I'm willing to settle on. But, the only way to prove that is for you to let go and trust me. Isn't that what this entire weekend was about?" He studied the rise and fall of her shoulders, then glanced to where she looked.

She gazed below at the meadow where blotches of deep blue wildflowers grew among the green landscape adjacent to the river. "Yes, but I'm scared to let go…of my heart." Sunrays painting her ponytail, wisps of her hair floated like the cloud puffs above.

He knew what he had to do, where he had to do it, right above where they'd stood among those unique iris bulbs that first day. "Do you trust me?"

"Yes, but…" her voice trailed off.

Under the weight of his palm, Jake felt her trembling shoulder quiet. All he needed was her momentary trust. "I'm not Steven. I'm not afraid of outcomes or endings. Curses. It's sharing that journey with the woman I love that intrigues me." Under his palm, he felt her still, but he kept talking. "Take that ride with me, Faith, like you did last night. Make now the start of a future…with me."

Moments passed, and high in the sky, an eagle soared, briefly casting its winged shadow across them.

"What are you saying?"

In the middle of the span, with her back to him, where he could not see the emotion in her eyes, he wrapped her waist between his legs. "Turn around. Face me, and see me like I see you. Because it's not you running that has kept me from sharing my feelings, but falling, Faith. Falling for you. Wanting you to take a chance on loving *me*."

"Love is abstract…it can't be measured."

He chuckled. "Yet, I'm filled with love. Let me prove how complete you make me feel, here, now."

Using his legs, she pivoted to face him, her eyes and mouth downturned. "I'm going to shame the hospital because of this, and my family, again. Something bad is going to happen. I couldn't stand if you got hurt."

"You deserve to be happy. We both do."

With her free hand, she held loosely to his knee that bent around her waist. "That's what Patti says, too."

"Patti is a good friend. Listen to her, like I listened to you." He cupped her face and thumbed her cheek. "Marry me?"

When she laughed, that beautiful melody

grabbed hold of his breath.

"You don't know what you're asking. Marrying me will test The Curse and put your life in danger."

"I'm hanging 300 feet in the air by a quarter-inch cable, and you think I'm worried about risk?"

She pushed down on his knee and tried to release her body, then relaxed. "I'm still worried….what if I ruin you?"

Pfft. He wasn't buying that. "In a mere two days, you've changed my life and made me see I'm a better man *with* you. I'm happier than I've been, because I believe in myself enough to choose when something feels right and when it doesn't. You taught me that. Trust me to be the man who will never let you down."

"We haven't known each other long." She reached forward and placed her hand on his cheek, stroking and encouraging him to press against her palm. "How can you be sure?"

He winked. "I'm trusting my instincts on this one."

"What are they telling you?" She bit her lip.

"All my life I've wandered, but now I feel like some fated link has brought me here. To you."

She glanced up at his connective cable. "You don't believe in the supernatural, remember?"

Meeting her gaze, he held those sky-blue eyes. "When it comes to you, I'd believe anything, as long as you say yes to becoming my wife."

Her eyes flooded until a shimmering stream flowed down her cheeks. "My parents won't take kindly to a weekend engagement."

"So, we give them a month." When he felt her hand drop away from his face, he added, "Maybe three months. Whatever you need. Just marry me, Faith."

"I can't let you lock into The Curse where escaping won't be an option."

He ran his thumb along her cheek. "Already, I'm under your spell. We're a dream team. Nothing we can't get through. I want you as my partner for life. For better or worse. Until death do us part, and then after."

She turned her head toward the distant platform, the guides waving her forward. "You don't know how unpredictable my future is."

Yet, that was the draw. The future was always tipping, a spinning top that could wobble, or gain speed, or completely collapse, only to rise once again. "No one does. And I don't care what the future holds, as long as you'll be with me."

She squirmed for a half-second, then settled against him, letting their jeaned legs and boots lace together. She wrapped her arm around his waist and held on.

Just the way he wanted to hold her.

"I-I—"

To keep her silent, he lowered his head and, in his kiss, loved her. Body overtook mind, heat blazed within him, and her subtle sighs only encouraged him to nuzzle her neck and inhale all that was this woman before him. "I love you, Faith. How so much so soon is a mystery, but nothing has ever been truer."

In his ear, she breathed, "I've never loved anyone more…so, yes. Yes, Jake, I will marry you."

He smiled both inside his heart, and deeper…instinctively, he pulled the band from his pocket, his hand trembling.

A glistening gaze met his. "Jake…I thought you said you weren't a Boy Scout?"

Slipping the ring on her finger, Jake noted the perfect fit. "My aunt would be smiling from ear-to-ear to see my beautiful fiancée wearing her ring…."

Holding the ring out so the platinum band caught the sunlight, Faith's breath quickened. "It's perfect. So perfect. Oh, my God, here we go."

Meeting his lips, they shared a long kiss. "Hold on, babe…hold on for dear life and never let go." He released both brakes and welcomed the rush of excitement into their future.

$\mathcal{E}$IGHT

AFTER THE RETURN home and meeting with the chief, Faith had agreed to stay put on the Dream Team. The chief approved Jake's probation early and even threw in a raise. Said he needed his Dream Team on a permanent basis. Since she'd agreed to marry Jake they'd been inseparable, and three months zoomed past. She'd learned the meaning of bliss and she smiled.

Today, however, was her day to prove by marriage The Curse would be broken once and for good.

Inside the mission church's bridal room, wedding day nerves zinging through her as quickly as her mother and Patti darted through the tiny room, she glanced into the full-length mirror. Blinking slowly, she stared at the pearled chiffon gown, satin shoes, and her grandmother's veil affixed to her up-do. Having finished with the photographer, she had a half-hour before guests arrived.

"You're gorgeous." Patti hugged her gently and handed her a blue garter belt. "I'm so happy to be your maid of honor. One day, you'll be mine…"

"I'd be flattered." Eyes watering, she slipped on the garter and smoothed her dress. "I couldn't be mad at you for long."

"Sometimes we need a little push. That's what besties are for." Patti gave Faith's cheek a quick kiss. "See you soon."

As Patti headed out, Faith picked up the deep blue iris bouquet, stems wrapped in white satin ribbon—

A pain shot through her hand and she dropped the flowers. Upon hitting her gown, the bouquet split and several petals scattered onto her train in dots of blue.

A rash of blisters quickly encased her ring finger and sent her stumbling backward. "No, no, no, no…this can't be. Not again. Not Jake."

"Let me see your hand." Faith's mother's rushed to her, worry clear in her pinched brow and narrowed eyes. "We have to hide this."

"I don't understand…" Faith breathed

deeply and held the breath tight inside. How could something be wrong when, until this moment, everything had felt so right? They'd performed several more "miracles" in the surgery ward. Her father had approved of Jake's protectiveness. Her mother was happy with Faith marrying a doctor. No surprise there. Jake proved his love both with words and actions. Now…this rash. "What should I do?"

Mama tossed her hands into the air. "We'll figure this out. Meanwhile, I'll get some ice. Maybe we can shrink the swelling, so the family doesn't have to undergo another catastrophe."

Faith scowled and her chest squeezed from her mother's blaming tone. Since the beginning, ever since meeting Jake, The Curse had been set in motion. There was no turning back for either of them…

A knock on the door made Faith jump.

"Hello?" Tori entered, holding a beaded wedding pouch. Her hair had begun to grow out, the two-inch length styled with decorative clips. "I wasn't sure if you had anything borrowed."

Accepting the beaded drawstring bag, Faith gazed at the pouch in awe. "It's so pretty. Thank you."

Tori squeezed the bag and it crackled. "I put a little something inside for your honeymoon."

Faith massaged her lips together and her eyes watered. "Thank you."

"I wanted you to know how special Jake is to all of us. He's such a welcome addition to this town. No telling how many others he's going to save." She palmed Faith's forearm. "You're a lucky girl. Truly as blessed as I've been. You know, Faith"—she leaned close, a meaningful look in her eyes as she lowered her voice—"I'm alive because I believed I was worth saving. Until my accident, I never realized how many people my life affects. Remember that…okay?"

Her friend turned to leave, and Faith examined the rash. Was she worth saving? Others' lives depended on Jake to save them. But, by continuing with the pending ceremony, she'd be putting his life in danger. And also countless others he might not be around to save.

Fog billowed outside the stained-glass window that Faith tried, hopelessly, to ignore. She just couldn't face what that fog meant. That thick fog that cloaked Whisper Cove and housed numerous Fog Spirits.

The mission bell tolled, the sound like

thunder that shot a bolt of pain straight to her heart. She sucked in air and clasped her mouth. The Fog Spirits were coming for Jake. No matter her good intentions, she'd put him in danger...not because she didn't love him, but because she did. Gathering her train, she gripped the chiffon in thick wads. Her chest squeezed until her throat choked with tears. She had to think, come up with a plan to save him, an elusive plan. To gather her thoughts, she knew just where to go.

Her pace quickened as she ran past the sanctuary pews strung with toile, ribbon, and iris bouquets. She threw open the double doors. Fog Spirits filled the streets like spectators at a homicide. Their cold mist sent chills up her neck. She didn't glance behind her, however, she glanced ahead, trying as hard as she could to outrun The Curse.

INSIDE THE GROOM'S room within the mission church, Jake was suddenly enveloped by a surge of nausea and he physically shook. To keep from falling, he clutched the mirrored bureau. While breathing in and out, he placed his palm over his heart, expecting the beat to be irregular and thready, but he found its rhythm steady.

Again, something struck from behind, and a chill rolled through him that he couldn't ignore. Wedding day jitters were normal. Marriage was a serious commitment he'd see through to the end of time. He wasn't having second thoughts or doubts.

The door opened, and a draft swept the room as the chief entered. "Wanted to wish you the best. Tell you how proud I am of you. You believe in yourself, anything is possible…." He cleared his throat. "I've been tough with you at times. I'm a proud man, as you must know. But, son, your commitment to everything you take on simply astounds me."

Sensing the chief was choked up, Jake shook his superior's hand then stumbled backward, that sick wave consuming him again. "Everything is happening so fast."

"Nonsense. Soon, a new phase of your life will begin." The chief's palm on Jake's shoulder tightened in a consoling squeeze. "Keep your focus on the future."

Only, something inside Jake's gut didn't feel like there would be a future. Quite the opposite. He glanced to the fogged windowpane. "Weather's changed."

The chief glanced out the window, his eyes widening before his gaze roamed over Jake. "Where's Faith?"

Where a moment before Jake could sense her, maybe even smell the sweet floral scent that was Faith, overhear her murmurs through the plaster wall that separated the two rooms and them both, he now realized those signs had disappeared. Something tugged him…no, pushed him as a chill shot through his body and pierced his chest.

He sucked an unsteady breath. Like the cable that had tethered him to the zip line, his connection to Faith seemed a tangible thing that should not exist, but did.

Faith's words came rushing back. *"The bloom lies in the hands of the propagator…we have the power to change the outcome. Believing in ourselves, that's where faith comes in."*

Hope welled in Jake's chest. "I'm Faith's propagator. I see her beauty, her worth, even though she cannot."

The chief tucked his chin, his voice low and deep. "Then you know what must be done…"

Jake's hands fell to his sides and the bowtie he'd been tying hung in two strands. Through sickness, poverty, or worse, he would profess to never give up on Faith, or their love, and he'd already promised all of those things in his heart since he'd proposed.

His compass to her spinning in all directions, he upped his pledge: Let no man or thing come between him and the woman he loved that he wouldn't rise up and see destroyed. Out the back door, he dashed toward Faith, to her aid, directly into the cold and chilling fog….

Note from the author:

I hope you enjoyed this prequel to Spirit Released. For the exciting continuation that leads to Jake and Faith's happily-ever-after ending, you won't want to miss reading *Spirit Released*, book 2 in the Whisper Cove series available at most retailers.

OTHER TITLES BY CYNDI FARIA

Whisper Cove Series
Spirit Awakened (Book 1)
Spirit Released (Book 2)
Spirit Embraced (Book 3)
Spirit Returned (Book 4)
Spirit Freed (Book 5)

Safe Haven Novella Series
Keep the Promise (Book 1)
Remember the Promise (Book 2)
Honor the Promise (Book 3)
Promises Collection (Books 1-3)

Visit Cyndi online at www.cyndifaria.com.

ACKNOWLEDGMENTS

As always, a huge thank you to my critique partners Susan Hatler and Virna DePaul who both inspire me every day by their amazing examples of dedication to the craft of writing. From the bottom of my heart, I thank Susan Hatler, whose critique suggestions and insights gave me plenty of laugh-out-loud moments, and helped me to weave in that heartfelt touch I look for in my characters. On this sometimes solitary writing journey, thank you Virna DePaul for inviting me to join you on one writing retreat after another, working through the night right along with me, and encouraging me to never give up. Love you girls!

A very special thank you to an amazing editor, Linda Carroll-Bradd, owner of LustreEditing.com, who sprinkles just the right amount of editorial magic into each book so the story shines!

Sending huge hugs to my hubby! He's my pillar! XO, Cyndi

ABOUT THE AUTHOR

Romance to Excite, Empower, Embrace.

"Faria's Whisper Cove series blends compelling suspense with an engaging romance!" –NYT and USA Today bestselling author, Virna DePaul

Award-winning and best-selling author Cyndi Faria was named an iBooks' Rising Star in Romance for her Whisper Cove series. She writes paranormal romance, contemporary romance, and romantic suspense to excite, empower, and embrace. She's also earned a BS degree in Civil Engineering and specialized in Humanities which helps her create page-turning plots laced with mystery and American folklore.

Cyndi joined Romance Writers of America in 2009. She's held the position of President of the Black Diamonds RWA Chapter and, currently, is VP Programs for Sacramento Valley Rose RWA with over 50 members. To date, she's indie published four novellas, three novels, and participated in two boxed sets, one a best-selling holiday anthology. In 2016, she'll introduce book

5 of her Whisper Cove series and launch a new gritty romantic suspense series.

On and off her sexy romance pages, this California country girl isn't afraid to dirty her hands fighting for the underdog and care for rescued pets. When Cyndi is not spending time with her fictional characters, plotting with fellow authors, or planning her next writing retreat, she's enjoying her family beachside, walking her furry family members, and gathering ideas for her next novel.

"(Cyndi Faria) has a talent for lovely happy endings and I'm so glad she does." –Night Owl Reviews

STAY CONNECTED WITH ME...

Facebook: www.facebook.com/CyndiFariaAuthor
Blog: www.cyndifaria.com
Twitter: @cyndifaria
Twitter: https://twitter.com/cyndifaria

Dear Reader:

Thank you so much for reading *Spirit Awakened,* Book 1 in the Whisper Cove Series and prequel to Spirit Released. As always, knowing you spent time with my courageous characters as they faced their inner demons and learned to trust their instincts, is what inspires me to keep writing. *Spirit Released,* Book 2 in the Whisper Cove Series and the happily-ever-after ending for Faith and Jake, is available now wherever books are sold.

Thank you so much for your tremendous support!

Wishing you peace and happiness always,
   Cyndi Faria